"I told you on the side of highway that you set my body on fire, and that you were going to have to put out the flames," he responds with a grin.

"Now wait just one damn minute. What happened on the highway was a moment of temporary insanity. I know you don't think that I'm just going to strip naked and jump in the bed with you?"

"Actually, I had envisioned stripping you out of your clothes piece by piece and enjoying the taste of each inch of your skin as it was revealed. Then I will lay you in the bed so you can watch me strip for you, before I make love to you with my hands, mouth, and then my body."

"Are you really a cop or are you some serial rapist or serial killer preying on unsuspecting young women on the highway?"

"I assure you that I am really a cop, and that I'm not a serial anything. Look for yourself," he states as he points to a bookshelf containing pictures of himself in basic training, graduating from the police academy, and various ceremonies where it appears he's receive numerous awards which are also displayed on the bookshelf.

After viewing all of this, the words he spoke finally sink into Zamora's mind, and her body gets hot all over at the images those words create in her mind. She shakes her head to clear her mind, "This is crazy," she states. "We don't even know each other, and will likely never to see each other again after this. I can't believe that you are even suggesting this."

"I know that you are right, but I still want you."

True Meditations of the Heart
Cleveland, OH
216-235-9803
Author.GStyl.com

First published 03/01/2011.

ISBN: 0615440843

Printed in the United States of America.

ReGina Crawford

Heart
Body
and
Soul

Published by True Meditations of the Heart
A division of G Styl Productions Incorporated

About the Author:
ReGina is a 43 year old divorced mother of three children 2 girls and 1 boy, ages 20, 16, and 5. She has been writing since the age of ten; beginning with poetry and short stories. Her first book, a romance novella, Triple Threat, hit the market in June 2008 with her second book, Food From The Heart, hitting the market in March 2009, and the response was overwhelmingly positive. Heart Body and Soul is her third novel, and is the third book in the series. She has had poetry published in five National Library of Poetry publications, and has also performed as the feature poet at other open mics in Cleveland and Columbus, OH, and her poetry can be heard on Blog Talk Radio on Saturday evenings on the show Wordplay Parley. She was featured in Who's Who in Black Cleveland in 2004 and 2009, and has received numerous awards for her contributions to the Cleveland Community, as well as, promoting entrepreneurship.

You can check her out on the world wide web at Author.GStyl.com, Facebook.com/GStyl, MySpace.com/GStyl, MySpace.com/GStylPoet, and GStyl.com.

Acknowledgements

To my three wonderful children, I love you more than words can say and I appreciate the love and patience that you given to me while I completed this book. Your faith and confidence in me mean more to me than anything in this world.

To my fans who have patiently waited for this book to be completed, thanks for pushing me to finish the book. I love you all.

To the many brothers and sisters whom have adopted me, and whom I have adopted as well, thanks for your love, support, and encouragement over the years. I love you all so much.

To Frost, my little brother and designer of all my book covers, thank you so much for giving life to my stories with your craft. For the cover draws a reader to the pages within. Love Ya Bruh

Characters:
Zamora "Czar" Richardson aka Zariah Robinson aka Zahara Umboto
Marquis "M&M" McMillian aka Marquise Markinson aka Pathfinder
Rick "Rock" Price aka Blackjack
Giovanni "GL" Lewis aka Giovanni Lawson aka Swamp Rat
Enrique "E-Dub" Whittmore aka Enrique White aka Sidewinder
Erik "E&J" Johnson aka Erik Jackson aka Excalibur
Sylvia "Snake Chaser" Williams

Language Translation:
One of the native languages of Senegal is Wolof

Wolof	English
Waaw	Yes
Deedeet	No
Numu demee?	How's it going?
Mu ngi dox	It's going
Naka nga tudda?	What is your name?
Laa tudda	My name is
Aajo ci dajee nga	Need to meet with you
Nuul ja minister	Black Market Minister

Heart, Body, and Soul

Though for years we've been apart,
You have always held my heart.
Even when I tried to push you from my mind,
And leave our love far behind.
My Heart, Body, and Soul belong to You.

Off we went with our dreams to pursue,
Of our future reunion we had no clue.
Apart would not stay our hearts and souls,
Over a love like ours there are no controls.
My Heart, Body, and Soul belong to You.

Once again our paths have crossed,
Once again to the wind caution we have tossed.
My heart, body, and soul are consumed with You,
To our love I'll forever be true.
My Heart, Body, and Soul belong to YOU.

~ReGina "G Styl" Crawford

This poem is dedicated to the man who claimed my Heart, Body, and Soul when I was 15 years old. I still love you to this day.
G

Instant Attraction

The red and blue lights suddenly flashing in her rearview mirror cause Zamora to curse like a sailor. As she eases her Emerald Green Mercedes to the side of the highway, she states out loud, "What the hell am I being pulled over for? I was doing the speed limit." After bringing the car to a stop, she looks in her rearview to watch for the officer's approach and what she sees when the cruiser door opens takes her breath away. Out steps an Ebony Adonis standing at least six foot three with a face meant to grace life-size billboards. His walk reminded her of the graceful cats of Africa from her trip two years ago. She feels her pulse begin to race, and it has nothing to do with the thought of getting a ticket.

She hits the button to roll down her window as he reaches her door. "Good morning officer," she states almost breathlessly.

"Good morning Miss. License and registration please."

She reaches for her purse on the seat beside her, and as she retrieves her wallet she asks, "Did I do something wrong? I know I wasn't over the speed limit. It's no secret that this stretch of highway is always monitored."

He simply cocks his eyebrow at her while reaching out his hand for her license and registration. After reading it over, he looks her directly in the eyes before saying, "Well if you know that Ms Richardson, why were you speeding through here last week?"

"Huh," is her shocked response.

"I was the officer you out ran last week while driving on this particular stretch of highway, and I have been waiting for your return."

She looks over his uniform for a name tag, and finding one she states, "I'm sorry about that Officer McMillan, but my Nana had a heart attack and I wanted to get to her before it was too late. I didn't want to waste precious time stopping for a ticket. Please accept my apology."

"So, how is your Nana now," he asks.

"She passed away that night, so you see how important it was that I get there quickly. I was her only grandchild, and my father was her only child and he passed on two years ago. I was her only family, I had to get there before it was too late."

"I'm sorry to hear about your loss. Were you able to get there in time?"

"Yes, she was awake when I arrived. Said she couldn't leave me alone without telling me good-bye. We spent the entire time talking about my antics as a child, and the antics of my father when he was a child. She said I was so much like him, and she wished that he was still here to look after me. I couldn't tell her how much I . . .," her voice broke off on a sob. The tears she held at bay for the past week rushed out of her along with body racking sobs.

"Oh hell," mumbles Officer McMillan before opening her door to pull her into his arms. "Shush. Shush," he whispers while cradling her in his arms. "You're going to make yourself sick if you keep crying like this." She only cries harder at his words, and he is at a loss as to what to say next. Suddenly she's wrapping her arms around his body tighter, like he is her only link to something solid. Her sobs have her body rubbing against his, and his body suddenly wakes up to the feel of her breasts rubbing against his chest and her thighs pressed tight to his. All the friction causes his manhood to become instantly alert and he knows he should pull back from her before she notices, but when he tries to untangle himself from her she only grips him tighter. Before he knows it, he is placing his hands on the sides of her face and kissing her for all he's worth. The sound of

2

honking horns reminds him that they are standing on the side of the highway in broad daylight.

"No," she begs as he breaks the kiss, and she tries to bring his lips back to hers. "Don't stop, I need this. Please."

He holds her at arm's length while trying to gain some semblance of control over himself and his out of control body. "I'm sorry," he states. "I just didn't know how else to get you stop crying. It wasn't supposed to go as far as it went." He steers her to the driver's seat of her car, and sees his clipboard along with her license and registration. Funny he doesn't even remember sitting them down. He picks them up as he helps her to sit down. He kneels down in front of her placing the items in his lap. He lifts her chin with his hand so that she is looking him in the eye, she instantly closes her eyes. "No you don't. Look at me."

She keeps her eyes closed and shakes her head while stating, "I'm so embarrassed. I can't believe I just did that."

Still holding her chin, he states once again, "Look at me."

Feeling like she might be fighting a losing battle, she opens her eyes and still sees desire in his. She closes her eyes again because she knows that same desire is reflected in hers as well. "Can't we just pretend like this didn't happen? Just give me my ticket, and I'll be on my way."

"No can do lady," he states. She opens her eyes and looks at him, her desire replaced by confusion. "You just set my body on fire, and I can't let you leave until you put out the flames." At the arching of her delicately arched eyebrow, he chuckles before saying, "You're going to get off the highway at the next exit, make a left, and then another immediate left. Pull up to the garage at the end of the road, and don't think about not following my directions since I'll be right behind you." He lets go of her chin, helps her get settled behind the steering wheel, and closes the door before jogging back to his patrol car.

Zamora starts up her car, and pulls into traffic. She wonders what the jail time would be for leading an officer on a high speed chase as she thinks, "I out ran him before, I could do it again." Then she notices her open wallet and remembers he didn't give her back her driver's license and registration. "Guess I don't have a choice now." She keeps looking in her rearview mirror as she drives, and sure enough he is right behind her.

When she reaches the garage, she turns off her car and gets out. She leans against her car with her arms folded across her chest as she waits for him to exit the patrol car and walk over to her. He notices her belligerent stance, but decides to ignore it as he grabs one of her hands and leads her to the house that goes along with the garage. Once he opens the door and ushers her inside, she turns on him with a quick spin, "Just what do you think is going to happen now," she asks hotly.

"I told you on the side of highway that you set my body on fire, and that you were going to have to put out the flames," he responds with a grin.

"Now wait just one damn minute. What happened on the highway was a moment of temporary insanity. I know you don't think that I'm just going to strip naked and jump into bed with you?"

"Actually, I had envisioned stripping you out of your clothes piece by piece and enjoying the taste of each inch of your skin as it was revealed. Then I will lay you in the bed so you can watch me strip for you, before I make love to you with my hands, mouth, and then my body."

"Are you really a cop or are you some serial rapist or serial killer preying on unsuspecting young women on the highway?"

"I assure you that I am really a cop, and that I'm not a serial anything. Look for yourself," he states as he points to a bookshelf containing pictures of himself in basic training, graduating from the police academy, and various ceremonies where it appears he's receive numerous awards which are also displayed on the bookshelf.

After viewing all of this, the words he spoke finally sink into Zamora's mind, and her body gets hot all over at the images those words create in her mind. She shakes her head to clear her mind, "This is crazy," she states. "We don't even know each other, and will likely never to see each other again after this. I can't believe that you are even suggesting this."

"I know that you are right, but I still want you."

"Listen Office McMillan," she starts.

"Marquise," he interrupts.

"Huh," she asks confused.

"Marquise. That's my first name. I think it would sound better if you yelled out Marquise instead of Office McMillan when you climax in my arms," he says around that ever present grin on his face.

"You are crazy. Look, Marquise, I don't want any trouble. I just want to go home get through my grieving period and then get on with what's left of my life."

"I would love to let you go, but I don't think that I should with the present state that you are in. What will it hurt for you to stay with me for a few hours? As you say we will probably never see each other again, and you can help me with my little problem and I can help you forget about your loss for a little while."

"What little problem," she asks skeptically.

"I haven't been with a woman in over two years, and honestly didn't have a problem with it until you wrapped your body around me on the highway. So, since you are the cause of my heightened state of arousal, I figured you could make it go away. Then I can go back to being content with being celibate, and you can go back to your life. So, what do you say?"

Instant Passion

Having never thrown caution to the wind before, Zamora decides to give in. Maybe this is just what I need to feel alive again. I won't have to worry about looking Nana in the face knowing that I am no longer a virgin without the benefit of marriage. "Okay, as long as we both agree that we will never seek each other out again after this."

He walks over to her and pulls her into his arms, "You have a deal," he states before lowering his mouth to hers. The sensations overwhelm the both of them, and he picks her up and carries her to his bedroom. True to his word, he begins stripping her out of her clothes. First her suit jacket is removed and laid over the back of a chair, then he slowly unbuttons her blouse placing hot little kisses on her neck, chest and stomach. Once he pushes the blouse off her shoulders, he kisses her collar bone, shoulders, and the swells of her breasts above her lavender colored ultra sheer bra. He then flicks his tongue over the turgid points of her nipples before removing her bra, at which point he tests their weight in his hands. He has large hands and her breasts completely fill them, and he is in heaven. He dips his head and takes one peak in his mouth to suckle. Her head falls back and a ragged moan slips through her lips. The sound encourages him to take the other peak into his mouth, and her continued moans are almost his undoing.

Not wanting to spill his seed inside his pants, he releases her breasts much to her objection and gets down on his knees as he unzips her skirt. Once the skirt pools at her feet, he helps her to step out of it and places it across the chair with her other clothing. He follows the line of her long legs up to the center of her which is barely covered by the lavender thong she is wearing, and has to close his eyes to regain control of the situation. Unfortunately, he takes a deep breath to steady his breathing and inhales the aroused scent of her which is causing his already straining member to press even harder against the front of his pants. Unable to hold back any longer, he reaches out and touches her between her legs. "You're wet," he says in a desire laden voice.

"More like drenched," she responds breathlessly as he continues to caress her through her thong. Unable to resist his touch, she spreads her legs wider to give him better access to her. At which point he slides a finger under the edge of her thong to caress her wet flesh, and an "Oh God," hisses from between her lips at his initial touch. She begins to tremble as her orgasm is fast approaching, "Marquise . . ."

"Yes baby, that's my name. Say it again."

"I'm about to cum," are the next words out of her mouth.

"Then let's get this first one out of the way," he responds while thinking it must have been sometime since she's been with a man since she's climaxing so quickly. Then all thought is gone as she yells out his name as her orgasm crashes down on her. "That's it baby. Just let it go. I promise you there will be more." As she rides out the final notes of her orgasm, he removes the thong, shoes and thigh high stockings. He lays her across the bed, and then begins removing his clothing. Once he is undressed, he climbs onto the foot of the bed and begins kissing his way up her legs from her ankles, steadily spreading her thighs wider and wider to accommodate the width of his body. Once he is settled between her thighs, he slowly runs his tongue across the center of her. She arches her hips up off the bed and closer to his mouth, and he takes full advantage of her position by taking her fully into his mouth.

"Marquise," she screams while clutching the sheets on the bed as her hips arch higher.

"Easy," he whispers while placing a hand on her stomach to keep her from going anywhere. "Easy," he whispers again letting his warm breath caress her. He then goes back to enjoying the taste of her. When he feels her ready to climax again, he whispers, "Let go baby. Feed me your love." Once his mouth touches her again, the orgasm crashes over her like tidal waves and she's screaming his name once again.

As she rides out this second orgasm, he covers himself with a condom from the nightstand drawer before rejoining her on the bed. Once she's breathing regularly again, he eases between her thighs and guides himself into her hot silky sheath. He meets resistance, so he withdraws and makes another attempt. Still more resistance, and this time he's sure it's not because it's been a while since she's made love. It hits him like a ton of bricks, she's a virgin. Damn! "Why didn't you tell me," he asks.

"Would it have made a difference," she asks in return.

"Hell yes it would have made a difference," he responds.

"Why? It's no big deal."

"Why? How can you ask why? Sweetheart, you waited this long to be intimate with a man, so I would say that it is a very big deal. Now, why didn't you tell me?"

"I need to have a connection to someone who is alive, and you are the person I've chosen. Plain and simple."

"There is nothing plain and simple about what we are about to do, believe that. And I believe that there is still something that you're not telling me." Tired of talking, Zamora arches her hips closer to him. The feel of her moving beneath him drains all thoughts from his mind, and his body takes over as he surges forward through the barrier separating him from her womb. He growls "Yes", as she releases a quick scream of pain as he buries himself to the hilt inside of her. Knowing this is her first time, he holds himself still giving her time to get past the pain of losing her virginity. "You okay," he asks after a few moments.

8

"I'm wonderful, but what are you waiting for," she asks as she flexes her inner walls around him.

The caress sends him over the edge, and he withdraws before surging forward once again. She quickly picks up on his rhythm and moves with him in the age old dance of man and woman. Their moans and sighs of pleasure fill the room as they frantically move to their destination of total fulfillment. The clutching of his manhood by her satin walls lets him know that she is ready to climax, and that knowledge brings him closer to his own release. He grips her hips in a tight embrace and strokes her for all he's worth. He can tell that this orgasm is more powerful than the first two, and that she is trying to run from it. "Don't fight it," is his hoarsely stated plea, "Come with me."

She follows his lead, and her climax has her screaming long and loud. His growl of pleasure as he finds his release mingles with her screams. Spent, he collapses on top of her, unable to move. Knowing that he must be crushing her, he rolls onto his side pulling her with him since he wants to stay connected to her.

Once his breathing returns to normal, he opens his eyes and finds that her eyes are still closed but she is wearing the most beautiful smile he has ever seen. "How are you," he whispers not wanting to startle her.

"There are no words to describe how I feel," she whispers her answer as she opens her eyes.

"I feel the same way. I have never felt anything that powerful before," he responds.

She closes her eyes and moans as an aftershock hits her, and she grips him as he is still inside her body. "Hmm," she moans at the feel of him.

"Be careful," he states. She intentionally squeezes him once again. "I don't think you know what you're asking for," he states. She squeezes him once again. "Remember you asked for it," he states as he feels himself lengthening inside her once again. He covers himself with a new condom before pulling her on top of him. At the question in her eyes, he guides her down on his throbbing manhood then grips her hips to show her how to move. She picks up quickly and begins moving on her own, sending his senses spiraling out of control. As she rotates her hips around him, he can take no more and quickly flips her onto her back never breaking the contact of their bodies. He then places her legs over his shoulders to give him greater access, and takes her on the ride of her life. Their labored breathing and skin making contact with skin are the only sounds to be heard throughout the room.

"Oh God," moans Zamora as her climax quickly approaches.

"Almost there," he growls in her ear.

"Yesssss," she screams as her orgasm hits her.

"Zamoraaaaa," he yells as he finds release once again. His body feels like rubber after both of his powerful releases, and once again he collapses on top of her. "Just let me catch my breath, and then I'll move," he whispers.

"You're just fine where you are," she responds while gasping for air.

Moments later, he rolls onto his side disconnecting his body from hers. She moans a protest at the loss of his body. He chuckles while still trying to regain control of the rapid beating of his heart and his breathing. "Lady, you are going to be the death of me," Marquise states some time later.

"What did I do," she asks.

"You know what you did."

"I have no idea what you're talking about. I'm a novice at this remember."

"That's right," he responds as he opens his eyes to look at her beautiful face. "But you're a fast learner, and I know you know that you have stolen every ounce of my energy."

"I know no such thing," she replies around her smile.

They lay there basking in the aftermath of their love making for another ten minutes before Marquise suggest that they get a shower. After finishing in the shower, they both dress silently knowing that their time together is about to come to an end.

As they reach her car, he reaches into his shirt pocket, and extracts a business card to hand to her. At her questioning look, "I know we said we would probably never see each other again, but just in case you want to get in touch with me take my card. My cell number is written on the back of the card." She starts to shake her head no, but he thrusts the card at her anyway. "Please, just take it. Even if you throw it away later, take it now."

She takes the card and places it inside her purse before turning back to him to give him one last kiss before she walks away from him forever. He doesn't try to detain her, he merely watches as she gets in her car and drives away out of his life. He's still standing there ten minutes after her tails lights have faded from sight. What is he supposed to do now? He has no idea, so he heads back inside the house since he wasn't officially on duty anyway today. He was just simply monitoring that stretch of highway in hopes that he would see the one that got away, and even though he captured her for a couple of hours she got away again this time taking more than just his pride. She took his soul.

Once she has put some distance between herself and Marquise, Zamora pulls off the highway into a rest area. She pulls his card out of her purse with every intention of throwing it in the trash, but she is unable to let the card go so she simply throws it into her glove box. With that done, she lays her head against the headrest and closes her eyes trying to regain some semblance of composure before she gets back on the highway. She

ReGina Crawford

wonders how long it will take the feel of him, the smell of him, the sound of him, the memory of him to fade from her mind, body, and soul.

Instant Recognition

Having just landed in Dakar in Senegal, West Africa, Zamora is tired and cranky but she must head straight to the FBI mock headquarters due to an untimely tie-up in customs. The car service delivers her and her luggage to the front door with only two minutes to spare, so slightly dragging she enters the offices and is directed straight to a conference room. A feeling of instant awareness hits both Zamora and Marquise at the same time. Zamora quickly scans the room to discover the reason for this feeling since she is sure she has never worked with any of the agents on this case before, and her eyes instantly collide with the eyes from her dreams as Marquise instantly looks in her direction. They both instantly register a look of shock on their faces before quickly masking their features before they are detected by anyone else in the room.

"Zamora," greets Head Agent Rick Price as he makes his way to the door, "Glad you finally made it." As he directs her to the only available chair which happens to be right next to Marquise, he states, "We were just about to begin the briefing." Introductions are made round the room before Rick gives the agents the details of why they are here in Africa. Once the briefing is complete, Rick turns to Zamora and asks, "Have you had a chance to check into the hotel yet?"

"Unfortunately, no. There was a tie-up in customs when I landed, so I came straight here from the airport."

"Well I'm sure one of the agents here can help you get to the hotel and settled in."

Before anyone else can respond, Marquise quickly speaks up, "I can get her squared away Rick since I believe that she will be occupying the room next to mine." He then looks her directly in the eyes, almost daring her to refuse his help.

Unbeknownst to Marquise, she is more than willing to let him assist her since she wants to know what the hell he is doing here on her assignment. "That sounds fine," she states more calmly than she feels.

The agents file out of the conference room on their way to the hotel, and Marquise spying her luggage picks up the cases as Zamora walks behind him sizing him up once again. Once he deposits her luggage in the trunk of his rental, he opens the door and assists her inside. He then jogs around the front of the vehicle and gets inside, before he can utter a word Zamora whispers fiercely, "What are you doing here?"

Marquise rolls his eyes and sighs before responding in an agitated voice, "The same thing you are doing here. I'm an agent on this case. When did you begin working for the agency?"

"I have been an agent for five years," she replies in an agitated voice of her own. "How do you go from being a small town sheriff to being an agent on this case in two years?"

Ignoring her question, he asks, "So you were with the agency the day we met on the highway?"

"Yes, and you were a small town sheriff," she responds with heat in her voice. "You still haven't answered my question."

Still ignoring her question, he asks another question of his own, "Why does a virgin FBI agent have sex with a man she meets on a highway in Georgia?"

"Why does a small town sheriff, who's obviously trying to become an FBI agent, have sex with a woman he meets on a highway in Georgia," she counters.

14

Running a hand over his head, Marquise takes a deep breath and exhales it slowly before glancing in her direction, "Look we are not going to get anywhere by antagonizing each other. Why don't we get you checked into the hotel, and then discuss our situation?"

Taking a deep breath herself, Zamora looks directly at him as she replies, "I agree. I'm tired and hungry, and I'm not trying to be difficult. Seeing you in that room after what happened between us two years ago was just a little unsettling, that's all."

They continue the ride to the hotel in silence, and maintain that silence while getting Zamora checked into the hotel. Once inside her room, Marquise orders room service while Zamora takes a hot shower. Once she is feeling refreshed and the food has arrived, they sit down to eat and continue their discussion. Since Marquise knows that she needs time to get adjusted to the new time zone, he begins to tell his story.

"I had already applied to the agency the day that we met on that highway in Georgia, and I didn't know that you were an agent. As a matter of fact, it took every ounce of control that I posses to not use my position as an agent to not look you up these past two years even though you invaded my days and especially my nights during all this time. But I was determined to uphold the agreement that we made that day. It was that day, after you left, that I got the call that I was accepted into the agency. I got this assignment since I excelled in every area of my training and field work since accepting the position, and I had no idea that you would be assigned to this case as well. Believe me when I say that our being here together is purely coincidental."

"Okay, say I believe your story," Zamora begins. Undeterred by his raised eyebrow, she continues, "How do you suggest we handle being on this assignment together? I know you have to still feel the attraction between us, and I don't want it interfering with the job we were sent here to do."

"I suggest that we act like adults who can control their libidos, and do the job we are here to do. I really don't think it will be a problem since we're both professionals trained to keep our feelings in check."

15

"I hope you're right about that," she mumbles.

"Why is that," asks a curious Marquise.

"Because seeing you again is making me feel things that I haven't felt since the day we met," she responds looking him straight in the eye.

"Oh hell," states Marquise as he closes his eyes. When he opens them again, he finds Zamora still looking directly into them. "Are you telling me that I'm still the only man you've slept with?"

"What? Do you find that hard to believe," asks Zamora with more than a little indignation in her tone. "Did you think that because I slept with you that I would suddenly start sleeping around?"

"Hold on," begins Marquise while holding up his hands, "I wasn't implying anything. It's just that it's been two years and you responded to me so passionately . . .," he falters at the angry look on her face. "Look, I'm not trying to upset you, it's just that I kinda figured once you discovered passion that you would find someone else to explore it with."

"Well I haven't," she huffs. Then somewhat under her breath, she states, "No one has moved me the way that you do."

"I'm sorry, what was that?"

"Nothing," responds Zamora as she gets up from the table to walk over to the windows.

Marquise walks up behind her and wraps his arms around her waist, "Zamora," he whispers near her ear and feels the tremor of her body. He closes his eyes and inhales a deep breath, "Baby, I know this is hard for you, but it's hard for me too. I never thought I would see you again, but now that you are here with me I still want you. Maybe even more than I did before, since I haven't been able to get you out of my mind, out of my soul."

Heart Body and Soul

Unbeknownst to Marquise, Zamora has closed her eyes and is replaying the events of that day two years ago in her mind, and is having the same thoughts as him. "I just wasn't expecting to see you again either, and seeing you is making me feel things I didn't think I would feel again," she states before turning in his arms. She looks into his eyes, and sees the same passion and desire in his eyes that she knows is showing in hers. "I don't know what to do with the feelings that I'm feeling. I've never been in a situation like this before."

"Damn," he mutters. "Please don't look at me like that. I'm already finding it hard not to take you to bed, and the fact that you want to be taken to bed is playing havoc on my senses." He feels more tremors from her at his words, "Aw hell," he states before he takes her mouth in an all consuming kiss. Zamora soaks up the kiss like the parched earth of Africa during the first rain of the rainy season. Consumed by the passion being transferred to her through the kiss, she moans and trembles in his arms. Once the need to breathe becomes unable to ignore, Marquise releases her mouth and they both gulp in air as their hearts continue to beat at a frantic pace. Marquise rests his forehead against hers while he struggles to pull much needed air into his lungs, but her trembling gets the best of him and he goes for her mouth once again. Unable to resist the magnetic pull of his mouth, Zamora responds with a desperation of her own as she returns the kiss.

Unable to hold out any longer, Marquise picks her up and carries her to the bedroom and lays her on the bed. Just like two years ago, they are both so consumed by the passion flowing between them that nothing else matters. He systematically undresses her as well as himself only taking his lips from her body to remove her shirt and his. Once he has her naked before him, he can't resist the urge to taste her core, and so he does causing Zamora to bite her fist to keep from being heard back in the states. As her hips jump off the bed, he places his palm on her stomach to ease them back to the bed so that he may enjoy the feast he's been craving for two years. His moans of ecstasy mingle with hers as he savors the taste of her, and he doesn't let up even when her orgasm crashes over her causing her to lift her hips off the bed once again.

Content that her taste is deeply embedded within his taste buds, he moves between her parted thighs to give her the ride of her life. The initial entry causes both of them to moan from the sensations it sends cascading through their bodies. Marquise pauses as he tries to regain some semblance of control over his heart, body and soul, but Zamora wants none of that and squeezes him with her internal muscles. Unable to hold back, Marquise strokes her at a hard grueling pace that has them both climaxing in no time at all. He muffles his growl in the space between her neck and shoulder, while she places her fist in her mouth to keep from screaming her joy. It takes them both a while to recover enough to speak let alone move.

"Baby, are you alright," asks Marquise as he rolls to his side a few minutes later.

"Mmmm. I've never been better," is Zamora's response as she places fleeting kisses across his chest.

"You keep that up, and there will be a second act to this play." Zamora responds by circling her tongue around his nipple before covering it with her mouth and sucking. "Oh shit," is Marquise's response, and Zamora moves to his other nipple. "You know you're pouring gasoline on an already blazing fire, right," asks Marquise as sensation after sensation grips his body.

"Just trying to make sure the fire doesn't die down or go out," quips Zamora while still kissing and licking across his chest.

He flips on to his back while pulling Zamora along to straddle his body, "There's no chance of this fire ever going out as long as you're around," he states as he places her silken sheath over his pulsating shaft. As she slides down further and further, Marquise moans and grips her hips in a firm hold. As she begins to rotate her hips in a circular motion, he begins thrusting upwards in an attempt to bury himself as far as he can within her womanly core. This round of loving is just as fast and furious as the first round as they try to make up for two years of doing without.

18

Heart Body and Soul

Dangerous Liaisons

Several hours later, Zamora and Marquise shower and dress before sitting down to talk once again. "You know that we are not going to be able to be together this way again while on this assignment," Zamora states.

"Yes, I'm aware of that," responds Marquise. "But we have a more serious matter to discuss."

"And what is that," asks Zamora while arching her eyebrow.

"The fact that we made love several times without benefit of a condom," responds Marquise.

"There is nothing to discuss," states Zamora.

"What do you mean there is nothing to discuss Zamora? You could have gotten pregnant."

"There is no chance of that Marquise since I've been on birth control for the past three months."

"If you haven't been having sex and weren't planning on having sex, why are you on birth control," asks Marquise trying to camouflage the anger he feels at her words.

"Standard agency procedure for all female agents when going on assignment in a country where the women are often kidnapped and raped," she states trying to mask the joy she feels at the anger he is trying to hide.

"Oh," states Marquise trying to feel taller than the inch her words reduced him to.

"Now, what do you suggest we do with the attraction that we have for each other," asks Zamora while Marquise tries to regain his composure.

Having somewhat recovered, Marquise replies, "We are both highly trained FBI agents who must maintain elaborate covers on a regular basis, I think we can maintain control over our bodies while we are here."

"Easy for you to say," Zamora mutters under her breath.

"I heard that," quips Marquise. "Let's just hope it is easy to do or this case is going to get infinitely more complicated than it already is."

"I'll do my part as long as you do yours, and I think we should minimize the amount of time that we spend together."

Knowing that will be impossible based on their roles on the mission, Marquise simply says, "It's time you got some sleep. Adjusting to the time zone change is quite a feat."

"I know. I've done it before," she replies. At his raised eyebrow, she states, "I was here two years ago right before we met." At his still raised eyebrow, she continues, "My parents died here two years ago, and I came to get some answers about what happened to them to no avail. However, I did find some information on some illegal activities while I was here, thus the reason we are here today."

"You're responsible for this investigation," he asks.

"In a way, but the jet lag is catching up to me, and I'll have to brief you on the details tomorrow," she states around a yawn.

"Okay," he states feeling somewhat responsible for her fatigue after the love making session they just engaged in. "Get some rest, and we'll talk more tomorrow." He kisses her on the forehead and leaves her to get some rest.

Once the door closes behind him, Zamora sinks down on the couch in the sitting room knowing that she cannot go back in the bedroom without replaying the acts of their love making. "This assignment is going to be harder than I first thought," she thinks as she closes her eyes and sleep overtakes her.

*****

Once back in his room, Marquise sinks on to the couch in his sitting area and places his head in his hands. "Get it together man," he states out loud to himself. "Why am I acting like a teenager with over-charged hormones?" He leans back on the couch letting his head drop back as he tries to formulate a plan to deal with having to be around Zamora on this assignment in an exotic location like Dakar, Senegal. "That day two years ago did a number on you man," he begins talking to himself again. "No woman has ever claimed your soul like the woman in the next room, and you better figure out how to handle yourself around her," he continues. "I know, I know," he responds. "Now I know I'm really losing it. I'm having a two person conversation with myself."

Unable to think clearly, he gets up and strips on his way to the shower. He can still smell her scent on his skin, and maybe if he can scrub it away he'll be able to think clearer. He stays in the shower until the water runs cold, however, he still can't get the events from two years ago and from the last few hours out of his mind. He knows that he will have to be focused so that he can do his job effectively, but right now he doesn't see how that is possible with the temptation of Zamora so close by. After his shower, he lays across his bed in nothing but a towel and falls asleep.

21

*****

Several hours later, Zamora wakes up a little disoriented and confused by her surroundings. When she tries to sit up, the aches in her muscles bring back the memories of her activities before falling asleep. She smiles as she remembers the pleasure that Marquise brought to her body, however, she knows that it cannot happen again while they are here in Africa. This assignment is going to be dangerous enough without her having to hide a liaison with a fellow agent. She is going to have to devote all her concentration on finding out what is really going on at IFAN, and hopefully find out what really happened to her parents. She slowly gets up from the couch testing the dexterity of her muscles, and finds that she is quite stiff after the long plane ride and her extracurricular activities. She decides to take a hot shower to try to loosen up her muscles, and to remove the lingering scent of Marquise on her skin.

Feeling refreshed after her shower, she unpacks her belongings and puts them away before sitting down at the desk to review the paper work she was given at the briefing. Since she is secretly heading up this case, she doesn't need to review the details of the case and concentrates on the background information on the other agents on the case. She and Rick have been peers for quite a few years, so she knows that he has picked agents she will be able to get along with, but more importantly he will have picked agents who are good at what they do and efficient.

As she reads their backgrounds and cover stories, she learns that Erik Johnson, or E&J as he is called, will be her apprentice to her cover role as an art curator. He is twenty-five and has just completed his Masters in African Art at Yale. Enrique Whittmore, E-Dub, will play her nemesis in an effort to discredit her qualifications and try to claim the art she plans to loan to the museum as fakes. Giovanni Lewis, better known as GL, will assume the role of a US Ambassador using her art donation as leverage to gain more favorable relations with the country's government. To her amazement and dismay, Marquise, who has been dubbed M & M, will be her security expert. "Damn, that means we will be working closely with each other while on this assignment," she states out loud. Then the thought hits her, he had to know this when he brought her to the hotel and made love to her.

Furious, she gets dressed and makes her way to his room. She is banging on his door in less than five minutes. A half awake Marquise opens the door to a glaring Zamora. She doesn't say a word, just barges her way into his room.

"Wake on the wrong side of the couch," he asks with his eyebrows raised.

Ignoring his question, she turns on her heels and hissed, "You knew what your role in this assignment was and you still made love to me."

He knew it wasn't a question, so he merely says, "And?"

"And? And? That's all you're going to say? And?"

"Czar, calm down," he begins only to be interrupted by her now raised voice.

"You don't get to call me that," she yells. "Only people who know me well get to call me that!"

"I think I know you better than anyone else at this point," quips Marquise with a knowing glint in his eyes.

Quickly discerning his meaning, Zamora's eyes narrow as her blood pressure continues to rise. "You know that is not what I meant at all," she hisses between clenched teeth before turning her back to him so that he doesn't see the effect his words had on her.

He walks up behind her and places his hands gently on her shoulders. He feels her flinch at his touch, and gently runs his hands up and down her arms from her shoulders to her hands. His voice barely above a whisper, he says, "Look, I'm sorry if I've upset you. That was not my intent. Nor was it my intent to make love to you today. When we were in your room,

23

I let my emotions get the best of me, but I promise I won't let it happen again."

Role Playing

He waits for her response as she takes several deep breaths, and he feels the tension slowly leave her body. "I guess if I want to be fair about this, I let my emotions get the best of me earlier as well." Taking several more deep breaths, she turns to face him. "It's just that this case is important to me since I'm the one who got the ball rolling," only admitting part of the reason this case means so much to her. She doesn't want anyone knowing that this case could be tied to the death of her mother and father.

"I get it. Don't worry, I'm sure we will be able to play our roles to perfection," responds Marquise hoping that he's telling the truth since he wants to make love to her again, right now.

"Thank you for understanding," she replies. She takes another deep breath before continuing, "I'm usually not this abrasive, but the implications of this case, the jet lag, seeing you, making love to you . . ." her voice trails off.

"Czar," whispers Marquise as he runs a finger across her cheek.

She closes her eyes, and takes several deep breaths before reopening them. The look in his eyes causes her to close her eyes once again as a shiver races down her spine. The things this man can do to her with a look, a simple caress should be illegal.

Once she opens her eyes again, Marquise speaks, "Everything is going to be okay. I promise to play my role and keep all my personal feelings to myself."

She puts a finger to his lips as she shakes her head, "Don't make promises you're not sure you'll be able to keep." When it looks as though he is going to respond, she presses her finger against his lips and shakes her head once again, "It's in your eyes. They're telling me that even though you mean what you say, it will be difficult for you to do. And I'm sure you see the same thing in my eyes. As I'm sure you know, I've never been in this position before, but I will try my best to keep my emotions under control when we are together. The people we are after wouldn't hesitate to use that information to their advantage, so we must be extra careful when we are together."

"As I said before, I get it. I had a copy of the brief for the plane ride over here, so I am aware of the delicate position that we are in while on this case. That is how I found out about your nickname Czar, and I must say that I am impressed by your wide range of fighting skills and knowledge of weapons."

"Thank you," she states somewhat shyly, not sure how she feels about the compliment that flowed so easily from his lips. "I wanted to take assignments all over the world, so I thought that it would be best if I learned some of the more successful styles of weaponless fighting, however, if in a situation where the use of weapons would save my life, I wanted to be able to use any weapon the enemy had on hand," she continues. "I have to admit that I didn't read the information on your background once I saw that you were my security expert, so you care to let me know what I'm working with?"

"While my background is not as extensive as yours, I was a Navy Seal for 20 years before being on the water 300 days of the year got to me. At which point I moved back home to Georgia, and immediately got picked by the Grandma Club to be the next Sheriff even though there isn't much crime in that small little town," he begins. "After about six months of no activity, I decided to apply with the Bureau. I knew it would take a while before I got word, so I continued on as Sheriff while I waited," he continues. "I had no idea that a beautiful, if lead footed, woman would come speeding down my stretch of highway or that I would find that I have developed a definite hunger for the taste of her skin."

"Marquise," states Zamora somewhat breathlessly at his words. "We have jobs to do, and roles that must be carried out to perfection. You can't throw out innuendoes like that, and expect me not to be affected. Remember, this thing between us is all new to me."

"I know, and I don't know why those words just came out of my mouth. Maybe it's the way the sun is hitting your skin through the window giving it this heavenly glow that just mesmerized me and made remember your taste on my tongue. I promise after tonight, I will have my emotions firmly in check in public. However, as for any private sessions we might have, well let's just say I plan to fully indulge myself in what has become my greatest craving."

Pulse racing, breathing labored, Zamora just stares at him unable to form a concrete thought as she replayed his words in her mind. The temperature in the room seemed to be climbing even though she knows no one has touched the thermostat. "I think I should just go to my room and read the briefing," she says a short time later after she managed to get her traitorous body back under control.

"Are you sure that's what you want to do," asks Marquise with a wicked smile on his face.

Unable to hold hers back, Zamora smiles in return, "Whether I want to or not, it's what I'm going to do," she states as she turns toward the door. "What I need to do if I plan on being able to walk tomorrow," she states somewhat under her breath.

"Feeling a little sore are we," quips Marquise. At the surprised look on her face as she turns back to face him, he states, "Yes, I heard that. Do you need a rub down?"

"I don't know if that's such a good idea considering the heat already simmering between us," she responds.

"Scouts honor, platonic rub down and nothing more," he replies. "You can trust me you know."

"It's not you I'm worried about," she states to herself.

"I heard that too."

"Damn, who are you Superman?"

"I'll be anything you want me to be.   Rub down or not?"

"Rub down, and I promise to behave," she quips giving him a sultry look over her shoulder as she walks out the door.

Marquise follows her to her room, and true to his word gives her the massage of her life. She falls asleep before he is even finished. Once he feels he has adequately taken care of her aching muscles, he makes his way back to his room and a cold shower before going back to sleep himself.

*****

The team meets for breakfast at FBI headquarters the next morning. Rick, or Rock as he is known in the agency, questions each one about the brief that they were to have reviewed the night before. He must be sure that everyone has their background stories straight, and memorized before they can begin engaging with the enemy. What no one in the room knows is that this assignment is even more dangerous than they perceive, and could lead to Zamora's death. Enrique thinks Zamora is a little too soft for this assignment, and begins antagonizing her in earnest during their role playing exercises.   He begins to get under her skin, and she lets her irritation with him show.

"Rock, are you sure she's the right agent for this assignment," he asks.

"I beg your pardon? How dare you question my abilities," she responds heatedly while poking her finger in his chest.

"I would recommend that you keep that finger to yourself," he states in a menacing voice.

"Or what," she asks while still poking him in the chest.

"Or this," he states as he makes a move to grab her wrist which she evades and promptly takes him down with a couple of Kenpo moves. Looking up at her from the floor, he nearly yells, "What the hell!"

"Still have doubts about my ability to handle myself on this assignment?"

Extremely frustrated and a little embarrassed, he grudgingly admits, "No, I guess you're well equipped for this assignment if you can take me down that quickly."

"Did you read the brief on her background last night," asks an amused Rock.

"I skimmed over it," he states as he gets to his feet. "I guess I should have read it in more detail then I would have known about her expertise with Kenpo."

Impressed that he knows the technique, Zamora assumes the respect stance and E-Dub does the same.

"Okay, now that you two are done marking your territory, can we get back the exercise," asks GL.

"Whatever man," states E-Dub.

They continue their role playing exercises for another four hours before Rock is satisfied that they are ready to begin the assignment they were sent here to do. Under the cover of nightfall, they each leave the compound one at a time to assume their roles.

Zamora and E & J are scheduled to be picked up at the airport in the morning by Marquise, so they head to Saint-Louis to catch their flight. Marquise will be heading to their hotel tonight to ensure that all security measures are in place for her and E & J's arrival tomorrow afternoon, as it custom for US security agents to arrive the day before the person they are protecting arrives. GL and E-Dub aren't scheduled to arrive for two days, so they leave the city so as not to be seen until then. Rock will remain at the compound to monitor everyone's activities including the people they are there to catch.

Heart Body and Soul

Mistaken Identity

As Zamora, or Zariah as she will be known on this assignment, and Erik make their way from the tarmac to the airport terminal, they see Marquise waiting for them looking every bit like the bodyguard he is supposed to be. He looks very imposing dressed completely in black, with his dark shades in place so that you can't see where his attention is focused. Once they reach his side, he makes a quick sweep of the tarmac before assisting them inside the terminal. As they reach the customs area to claim their luggage, a very aged man drops to his knees in front of Zamora and begins sobbing, "Princess Zaraha, you have returned to your home land. We thought you met the same demise as the King and Queen when they returned home two years ago. You must be careful child, those that killed your parents will kill you too if they see you. You must go underground and quickly."

Somewhat overwhelmed and greatly confused, Zamora addresses the elderly gentleman, "I'm sorry sir, you are greatly mistaken. My name is Zariah Robinson, and I am an Art Curator from the US. I am not this princess you speak of."

"That's good, keep your cover. Be extremely careful when arriving at the kingdom, there are traitors to the crown everywhere."

"Sir, again, I am not this princess you speak of, and I will not be traveling to any kingdom while I am here."

Marquise grows extremely tired of the conversation, but knows that he must not offend anyone. So he gently helps the man to his feet, and says, "Sir, I'm afraid the lady is quite right. You have mistaken her for your princess. I assure you that she is an American citizen here in your country to do business with your museum. Now, we are running late and must get moving. Take care," he concludes as he gently but insistently ushers the man away from Zamora.

After they have retrieved their luggage and are heading towards their waiting limo, they run into a group of market women who also drop to their knees sobbing, "The princess has returned, the princess has returned. We knew you would not forsake your people after the assassination of the King and Queen. We knew you would come."

"Okay, this is going to be a problem," states Marquise somewhat under his breath. As he tries to usher Zamora into the waiting limousine, however, she doesn't appear to be in any hurry to get inside the waiting vehicle. "Czar, we can't stop and talk every time this happens. We will have to deal with this later."

Understanding his meaning, Zamora moves around the kneeling women and gets inside the limo. "That is so weird," she states sounding somewhat dumbfounded by these latest events. "I've been here before, and no one reacted to me this way then. I don't get it," she states.

Having been quiet this whole time, Erik states, "This could present a serious problem for us while we're here. If there is some type of coup being planned in the kingdom of this missing princess and everyone thinks you're her, we could have more bad guys on our tail than originally planned."

"Quite right E & J, I'll let Rock know about this development once I have secured the two of you at the hotel. And I'm thinking that you should cover your features with a shroud when out in public from now on to keep this from happening. We do not need to draw unnecessary attention to ourselves while we're here," states Marquise.

"I know you're right," states Zamora while deep in thought. What the other occupants of the limo don't know is that her parents were killed in this city two years ago, and she is wondering if her parents were mistaken for this king and queen the natives speak of and that's why they were killed. Is it possible that her parents resembled them and she resembles their daughter? This is too much for Zamora to absorb all at once, and she remains quiet for the rest of the ride to the hotel.

Marquise at once picks up on the uncertainty that Zamora is feeling, and watches her very closely during the ride. He thinks to himself, something about those events is really bothering her, and he can't fathom why. He intends to get to the bottom of it though, just as soon as he can get her alone.

Once they arrive at the hotel, Marquise sticks closely by Zamora's side and tries to shield her face from the people around them as much as possible to prevent anyone else for mistaking her for this missing princess. He doesn't even wait for her luggage to be unloaded from the car, and E & J having picked up on the tension in the limo doesn't mind handling that duty.

Since Marquise checked in yesterday, he already has the room keys, so there is no need to stop at the front desk and he escorts Zamora straight to their suite of rooms. Once she enters the room, she heads straight for the bathroom off her bedroom and closes the door behind her. Not wanting to add to the distress that he saw on her face, Marquise lets her have her space for the time being.

Ten minutes later E & J knocks on the door with the luggage at his feet a little pissed because he didn't know what room they were in, and the clerk at the front desk wanted to do a complete background check on him before giving him the room number and a key to get in. Seeing the pissed look on his face, Marquise arches his eyebrow at him in a questioning manner. Erik doesn't bother to answer the question on Marquise's face, and simply gestures to the luggage he has sat at the front door. That's when it dawns on Marquise what is bothering the young agent.

"Sorry man, I just wanted to get Zamora out of the public eye as quickly as possible after what happened at the airport."

Erik lets go of some of his anger at the apologetic look on Marquise's face. "The only problem I had was getting the room number," responds Erik.

"Oh shit," states Marquise.

"Which wouldn't have been a problem except the clerk at the front desk practically did a full out background check on me before she would give the room number and a key."

"Damn, sorry about that man. She was told that anyone who needed to know what room we are in wouldn't have to ask for the room number."

"It's cool man. I know what happened at the airport was unexpected. By the way where is the princess?"

Marquise arches his eyebrow in a not too friendly manner, to which Erik raises his hands in mock surrender. "She went straight into her bedroom when we entered the suite and hasn't come out since. I'm beginning to get worried about her, but I don't want to invade her space."

"I feel you man, but I think someone should check on her and I'm willing to let that be you. I'm going to go down to the bar so that she won't feel too crowded," states Erik as he heads for the door to the suite.

"Shit," whispers Marquise. "This is the last thing that we needed. Zamora and I in close proximity with her in a highly emotional state. Shit," he hisses again as he heads to her bedroom door. He knocks gently. No answer. He knocks a little harder, and still no answer. He calls her name, and still no answer. Becoming concerned and agitated at the same time, Marquise opens the door, doesn't see her, and enters the room. Once he
34

reaches the bathroom door, he stops dead in his tracks. Zamora appears to be sleeping in the tub and all of her bubbles have evaporated if there even were any in the first place. His breathing immediately becomes labored as he takes in her six foot one inch frame surrounded by shimmering water. Her breathing is even, but he can't help but notice how her ample breasts are moving up and down with the rhythm of her breathing. He watches the water loving caress her ample hips and shapely legs, and feels his manhood strain even harder against the zipper of his pants. "Damn," he whispers, "this is the last thing I need." Knowing he would soon not be able to resist the urge to join her in the tub and join with her, he turns and walks back out of the bathroom to find a drink of his own.

Once the door closes, Zamora opens her eyes and just lies there staring at it. After five minutes of just staring at the closed door, she gets out of the tub, dries off and puts on one of the hotel robes. She enters the sitting area of the suite and sees not a soul, but she does spy her luggage by the front door. Wanting to be dressed before the men return, she takes her luggage into the bedroom and begins to unpack. A half hour later her task is complete, and the men haven't returned. Feeling hunger pains, she decides to get dressed and do something about her growling stomach. Just as she finishes fastening the clasp to her bra, the door to the room opens and Marquise pokes his head inside.

"Shit," he hisses as he closes his eyes to the image of Zamora standing there tall and regal in a royal purple bra and panty set that is so see-through she might as well be wearing nothing at all. He opens his eyes to see that she hasn't moved an inch except to place her hands on her hips, which just makes her look even sexier than she did when he first poked his head into the room. He steps all the way into the room, and closes the door. She still doesn't move, so he slowly walks over to where she is standing and circles a finger around her already hardening nipple. Other than closing her eyes, Zamora still doesn't move. Marquise then takes that same finger in his mouth before circling the other nipple. He can't help but notice her heightened breathing at his touch, and smiles that devastatingly sexy smile of his. "If you don't want me removing the next to nothing that you're wearing and taking your beautiful breasts in my mouth, I suggest you cover up," he quips around his smile.

35

Surprisingly, Zamora returns his smile as she quips in return, "What if I don't like your suggestion?" He raises his eyebrow at her, so she continues, "What if I want to feel your hot, wet mouth on my breasts?" Marquise closes his eyes at her words, and takes several deep breaths trying to get his body under control. Zamora takes advantage of his eyes being closed, and leans over and runs her tongue across his lips. His breath catches in his throat at the feel of her tongue, but he quickly recovers and captures her tongue with his own. Zamora abandons herself in the kiss, and that is all it takes to send Marquise over the edge.

He picks her up and carries her over to bed, and lays her down on it. In no time at all, he has them both stripped naked and is riding her for all he's worth. They both climax quickly, but their recovery is much slower. Once their breathing returns to normal, Marquise looks her in the eyes and asks, "Why did the events at the airport bother you so much?"

Zamora closes her eyes and tries to withdraw from him, but he's not having it and wraps an arm and a leg around her. He doesn't say anything more, just patiently waits for her to open her eyes and answer his question. A short time later, she complies by opening her eyes and saying, "It's probably just a weird coincidence, but two years ago my parents were killed in this very city. And when those women said that the king and queen were killed when they returned here two years ago, it freaked me the hell out. My parent's death was an accident according to the authorities here, but I couldn't help but remember some of the inconsistencies in the reports we received at the bureau about their death."

"What inconsistencies," asks a curious Marquise.

"It's probably nothing," she responds.

"What inconsistencies," he asks again.

"Well, they weren't supposed to be on camel ride in the middle of the desert the day they were killed. And I have never heard of camels getting spooked by snakes the way horses do, so it just seemed odd that the spooked camels took off at a fast pace and ran right off a cliff killing themselves as well as my parents."

"I've never heard of that happening either," states Marquise. "Was a thorough investigation done into the incident?"

"Yes. That's why I was here two years ago. I wanted to make sure that the local authorities here cooperated completely with the investigators from the local embassy here. We found nothing amiss in the autopsies of my parents or the animals, so we agreed that it was an unfortunate accident."

Their conversation is temporarily put on hold as they hear Erik enter the suite. Figuring he was probably going to head straight to his room to unpack, they didn't panic but did get up and get dressed.

Curiosity and The Cat

Just as Zamora is putting on her shoes, her stomach lets out a hungry growl reminding her of why she was getting dressed before Marquise entered the room. Marquise, putting on his shoes as well, bursts into laughter at the mortified look on her face. "This is not funny," she huffs before bursting into laughter herself. Once they recover from their laughter, she adds, "That's why I was getting dressed in the first place, I was hungry."

"Why didn't you say so when I first walked in here," he asks.

"It seems another hunger overtook the hunger of my stomach, and I decided to satisfy that hunger first."

"Damn it Zamora," hisses Marquise as he feels is body start to harden. "You can't say shit like that."

"Why not?" He doesn't respond, but simply stands up in front of her. "Oh," she responds trying to stifle her laughter at his aroused state. "You might want to do something about that before we leave this room," she states in a sultry voice.

"Don't start," Marquise nearly growls. Zamora leans back on the bed, and gives him the most seductive look she can. "E & J is just on the other side of the suite, and I don't plan on giving him a reason to come barging in here, cause lady if I do what you're suggesting I'm going to love you so well they will hear you screaming all the way back to the states. Now let's go feed your growling stomach."

Ignoring his last words, Zamora states in a sultry voice, "I would love to feel you make that happen."

"Enough lady," states Marquise as he walks to the door and opens it. Zamora starts laughing, and Marquise sees Erik coming out of his room. "Hey man, we're about to go get something to eat once the lady here gets over her fit of laughter."

"I'll be there in a minute," she states through her laughter.

Marquise walks into the sitting area to join E & J. "I'm glad you got her to laugh," begins Erik. "I was really worried about her on the ride here from the airport. Something about those people mistaking her for a missing princess really freaked her out."

"I know, but she's okay now. So, after we get something to eat, we can go over our roles and schedule for the next few days."

"Cool. I have to admit this is my first full-fledged mission, so I'm a little nervous. The art stuff is a walk in the part, it's the villains we're after that I'm a little nervous about."

"Don't worry about it. You're here to get your feet wet on a mission, GL, E-Dub, Rock, Zamora, and I will handle the more intricate stuff. You just watch and learn, and pretty soon you'll be an old hand at this game of subterfuge that we play as agents."

"I plan to learn all I can while I'm here. I'm just thankful that my art background has proven useful." Zamora walks out of the room at that moment, and both men turn in her direction. "Wow," states Erik.

"I know. I know," replies Zamora, "I look like one of the natives of this country with this get up on, but I don't want any more people mistaking me for their princess."

The three of them head down to the hotel restaurant to have dinner, and are thankful that no one approaches them as they walk through the hotel lobby. After a quiet but pleasant dinner, the three of them make their way back to their suite to go over their plans.

Once they feel like they have all their bases covered, Erik heads to his room to get some rest. Zamora and Marquise remain on the sofa drinking coffee and just looking at each other. Finally Marquise says, "You know what happened in here this afternoon can't happen again while we're here, right?"

"I know, but I don't know how to control how you make me feel," she replies.

"I know this is new to you, but sweetheart you're going to have to stop tempting me," he responds.

"I'm not tempting you right now."

"Yes you are."

"I'm not doing anything."

"You may not think you're doing anything, but the way you are looking at me says volumes."

"And just how am I looking at you?"

"The light of desire is shining brightly in your eyes, and you have the sexiest pout on your lips that is just begging me to kiss you."

"Damn," she whispers.

"What?"

"I was just sitting here thinking about how well you kiss, and not only the lips on my face."

Marquise closes his eyes at her words as his body readies itself to make love to her again. "Damn it Czar didn't I tell you about saying shit like that?"

"I'm sorry. Maybe I should go to bed now."

"Yes, that's a good idea," he states as he stands on his feet. "I'll see you in the morning, sweet dreams," he adds as she stands up and heads towards her room.

"I'm sure they will be," she says with a wink as she walks into her room and closes the door.

Marquise hears her laughter as he heads in the direction of his room talking to himself, "That woman is determined to drive me crazy." He shakes his head as he walks into his room, "Look, I'm already talking to myself again." Once inside his room, Marquise opens his laptop and begins searching for information on Zamora's parent's death and the missing royal family. What he finds makes the hairs on the back of his neck stand up. He still has connections with a few active Navy Seals, and a couple of them are in this area. He opens the secret compartment of his suite case and retrieves the phone he keeps there for situations such as this, and gives one of them a call.

After two rings the phone is answered, "Cockroach."

"Pathfinder here."

"Wow. Must be serious."

"It is, and above top secret."

"Gottcha."

"Need info on a missing African Princess and her family. Umboto. Zuriel. Zawadi. Zahara. Two clicks."

"Two clicks."

The line goes dead, and Marquise gets undressed and heads for the shower. Once he has completed his shower and gets dressed, he sits back down at his laptop to review the data he found on Zamora's parents. They were both antiquities dealers specializing in African Art from this region. They seem to have extensive knowledge about the art, and had in their possession extremely rare pieces from the region that mysteriously disappeared around the time the King and Queen fled the country during a hostile takeover by a neighboring kingdom. They were in the country consulting with the curator of Institut Fondamental d'Afrique, one of the oldest art museums in West Africa, about purchasing some of the art work. It seems the curator wasn't too pleased about them possessing the art work, and alerted the authorities about it. Yafar and Yamina were not being detained by the authorities, nor were they being given permission to leave the country either. As a result of their inability to leave the country, they decided to explore more of the country, and hired a tour guide to take them to some of the outer regions of the country that were accessible by camel only. They were actually headed towards the kingdom from where the royal family had fled some twenty-eight years ago, and that is when and where their accident occurred. While the official report doesn't indicate that there was any foul play involved, Marquise's hair is standing up on his neck and he never ignores this warning sign that something is amiss.

Two clicks later, he's read everything he can get his hands on and places the call he's been dying to make.

"Cockroach", states the voice on the other end of the line.

"Pathfinder here."

"What the hell have you gotten mixed up in now," asks the voice on the other end of the line.

"Not sure. Need more info."

"The Umboto kingdom contains some of the most lucrative diamond mines in this part of the country, as well as, some of the most fertile land. It is highly coveted by the ruling family of an adjoining kingdom, and they tried to gain access by getting the Umbotos to agree to marry their first born child to one of their children. When the Umbotos did not agree to the marriage contract, the Gambotos staged a hostile takeover of the Umboto kingdom. Since the Umboto kingdom did not have a large army, they were not equipped to fight for their land and were almost taken over. However, the authorities stepped in and stopped the takeover, but then several attempts were made to kidnap the Umboto Princess Zahara who was only two weeks old. It was then that the African authorities contacted the US about providing asylum to the family until the child became of age, however, the plane they were supposed to be on crashed in the ocean and no bodies were recovered. So it was believed that the entire royal family perished in the crash, and the African government has been ruling the kingdom ever since. Over the years there have been continuous attempts by the Gambotos to gain control of the land."

"Damn," hisses Marquise.

"Yes. Now what's going on?"

"Still not sure, but I may have the missing princess in my protection. Only she doesn't know that she is a princess."

"What?!? Are you serious?"

"Deadly."

"Here if you need back up."

"Thanks. Don't be surprised if you hear my war call."

"Won't be."

The line goes dead, and Marquise curses a blue steak through the room.

Naja Melanoleuca (Forest Cobra)

A phone rings in a darkened room.

"Waaw," asks the voice on the line.

"Aajo ci dajee nga."

"Naka nga tudda?"

"Nuul ja minister."

"Is she here?"

"Yes, and we need to get her taken care of as soon as the documents are signed."

"We'll meet at the usual locale."

The line goes dead, and the caller heads to the assigned meeting place. Upon his arrival, he doesn't see his contact and starts to get angry. "Damn Africans are always late!" Suddenly the wall in front of him separates, and he nearly jumps out of his skin.

"I assure you Monsieur, I am never late. I had to make sure that you were not followed as you Americans are too impatient and never careful enough in your travels."

"Whatever," huffs the American. "We need to make sure that the artifacts are going to make it to this country this time. I can't afford to have any mishaps this time."

"Surely you are not blaming me or my people for what happened the last time," responds the African contact. "Your people jumped the gun last time, and killed the Richardson's before the locale of the artifacts was known."

"That's neither here nor there at this point," states the American. "Once I find out how the artifacts are going to be delivered, I will need your people to be ready to retrieve them before they make it to customs and deliver them to me."

"My people will be ready," the African states with confidence. "You just make sure that you have the necessary paperwork to prove that the Robinson woman is not the rightful owner of the artifacts so that my country my gain control of them."

"The paperwork is already complete. You just make sure that you have my money when I deliver them, and make sure that her death looks like an accident."

"There was no foul play detected with the Richardson's deaths, and there will be none detected in this young woman's death either."

"There better not be! Now layout the plan for me so that I can make sure that my connection to you is not found out, or that I am in any way responsible for her death."

The two sit down to go over the plans already put into place to steal the artifacts, and get rid of the woman who has them in her possession.

Once he is sure that everything is in place for the mission, the American takes his leave. As soon as he is out of sight, the same wall separates again and two more men emerge into the room. "Make sure that he is taken care of as well when this deal is complete," states the American's contact. "Uppity ass American Negro!"

"We will take care of him boss," state the two henchmen at the same time.

They all take their leave of the hideaway, and put their plans in motion.

*****

The American, believing that his intellect is far more superior than those of his African counterparts, is none the wiser of their plans to assassinate him as well as the American woman. He is too busy making plans of how to hide the money he will receive from this deal, and planning his retirement to parts unknown. He is tired of working for the American Government and not receiving the recognition that he feels he rightly deserves.

Upon arriving back at his villa, he contacts his forger to make sure that the paperwork is indeed complete and looks genuine.

The person on the other line states, "I assure you Monsieur that the paperwork looks authentic, and no one will be able to question the legitimacy of the papers you will deliver to the African Museum."

"They better not! I will let you know when I am ready to pick up the papers, and make sure that the security around your place is up and working! I don't need anybody seeing me arriving and leaving your place!"

"I assure you that my security is top notch! How do you think I have been able to remain in business this long? As well as create documents for every country in the world? You just make sure that no one is following you when you travel here!"

"I am a highly trained American Spy! I know how to travel undetected," states the agitated American. "I've had to wait two years to get my hands on these artifacts again!"

"You don't have the artifacts yet."

"As long as you people don't screw it up this time, I will have them and I will get my money!" Agitated beyond belief, the American slams his phone closed.

"Damn Africans get on my nerves," he all but growls. "I just know they better get it right this time!"

He then begins his preparation for the role his government sent him here to play. He prays that his true feelings do not emerge when he encounters the American woman who has made his plans to get his hands on the artifacts difficult for the past two years, and who almost discovered his identity two years ago. He still hasn't been able to find out what her connection to the Richardson's is, and as much as he wants to know he wants to get his hands on those artifacts more. He stands to make enough off of this deal to buy a small island, and live out the rest of his days in pure luxury.

"Still I would love to know how Ms Zamora came to have the artifacts in her possession," he says out loud to himself. "My government contacts became a little too suspicious of me when I asked about it before, but maybe the role I'm currently playing will get me some answers," he continues. "Hmm. . . I'll have to make some calls."

*****

"Damn Americans! Always thinking that they are so superior to us," states the forger. "It would serve him right to lose out on the artifacts this time around as well."

Heart Body and Soul

Shadows

The following morning, Marquise is on high alert as they leave their suite of rooms to head to the museum, and he does his best not to make it obvious to Zamora or Erik. When the rented car stops in front of IFAN, Marquise exits the car first to check out who's in the vicinity before he allows Zamora and Erik to exit the vehicle. He swears he sees the shadow of someone at the building across the street, and he feels the hairs stand up on the back of his neck. Just as he adjusts his eyes to the bright light of the sun, the shadow disappears. He peeks his head back inside the car to make sure that Zamora's shroud is in place, then helps her out of the car. He wastes no time getting her inside the museum leaving Erik in their wake. Once Erik catches up to them, he arches his eyebrow at Marquise and the look that Marquise gives him in return lets him know to leave it alone for now.

The museum greeter walks up them with a smile, "Welcome to Institut Fondamental d'Afrique Noire," she states in such a heavy accent that Marquise and Erik barely understand what she has said.

"Thank you," replies Zamora. "I am Zariah Robinson and this is my apprentice Erik Jackson. We are here to see Monsieur Orogotto."

"Monsieur Orogotto only sees people by appointment," responds the young lady in a somewhat superior voice once she realizes that they are American.

"We have an appointment," states Zamora in the same superior voice. "We are here from the United States with important business to discuss with the Monsieur."

Before the young lady could respond, Monsieur Orogotto walks into the foyer of the museum. When he spots Zamora, a look of surprise registers on his face before he has a chance to mask it, and Marquise being on high alert doesn't miss it. He walks over to where they are standing, "Do I know you," he asks in perfect English.

"I am Zariah Robinson from the United States here about the art left behind after the passing of Yafar and Yamina Richardson," responds Zamora.

"Ah, yes, yes. Please come to my office," the curator states as he takes Zamora by the arm and leads back the way he came leaving Erik and Marquise to follow in their wake. "It is such a pleasure to finally meet you," he states as they walk down a long corridor. "We have spoken on the telephone many times about the artifacts in your possession. I can't wait to see them, and see if they are indeed genuine," he continues talking at a mile a minute. "I was so pleased to hear from you, and that you would even consider letting the art work return to its native country." He pauses to take a much needed breath before continuing, "I was afraid that they were lost to us forever after the tragedy that befell the Richardsons when they were here. It's more than passing strange that a few of the natives mistook them for the missing King and Queen of Umboto. I think that them having possession of the art work is what caused the people here to believe that they were the King and Queen. You know the art work which you claim to have in your possession where personal pieces of the royal family."

He finally stops talking as they reach the door at the end of the corridor. He opens the door, and leads Zamora to a chair in front of his desk. Erik and Marquise enter right behind them with Erik taking the chair next to Zamora and Marquise standing at attention by the door. Marquise surveys the room for alternative exits, and possible hiding places for spooks. Unbeknownst to him, Erik is doing the same, and so is Zamora.

After Monsieur Orogotto takes his seat behind his desk, Zamora coolly states, "I do have in my possession the artifacts of which we spoke of over the phone. I was the Richardson's apprentice at the time that they traveled to this country to present you with their proposal for returning the art work to this country and your museum."

"I did not mean to offend you Femme Robinson. However, since I never received proof that the Richardsons actually possessed the pieces, I have no proof that you have them now."

"Of course," responds Zamora. "Forgive me. It was a long trip, and I am still adjusting to the time change."

"Of course," he responds.

As Zamora reaches into her sack to retrieve the agreement drafted by her parents, she sees Erik in her peripheral vision. "Please forgive my bad manners Monsieur," she begins before turning towards Erik, "This is Erik Jackson my apprentice. He received his art degree from Yale. He has a great passion for the art work from your country, and especially this region."

"Monsieur Jackson," greets Orogotto, "Please forgive my bad manners as well. I am so excited about finally being able to see the art work, that I did not acknowledge your presence."

"Monsieur Orogotto," greets Erik in return. "I understand your excitement for I was just as excited when Femme Robinson chose me to be her apprentice on this trip." Both men grin at each other in understanding as Zamora once again reaches into her sack to retrieve the agreement.

*****

While Zamora handles the job she was sent to do, Marquise makes mental notes to thoroughly check out the young lady that greeted them, as well as, Monsieur Orogotto. The look on the young lady's face, when Zamora announced who she was, was a mixture between hate and calculating. The Monsieur looked at her as though he thought he knew her, and Marquise wonders if he recognized her as the missing Princess. His endless chatter bordered on nervousness as well.

Erik is making some mental notes of his own as he observes the interaction between the curator and Zamora. When he thinks no one is looking at him, he has a look on his face that doesn't sit well with Erik and he too is wondering if the curator thinks that Zamora resembles the missing Princess. Something about the whole situation doesn't sit right with him, but he hasn't done this long enough to have the instincts that Marquise has.

*****

Zamora retrieves the agreement and lays it on the curator's desk, "The terms of the agreement have not changed from when the Richardsons originally drafted it two years ago," she states as he picks it up to read.

"Really," states the curator with what appears to be surprise in his voice. "The Richardsons wanted the artifacts returned to them in one year if it didn't bring political rest to the country. Who will the artifacts be returned to now if that doesn't happen?"

"To me of course," states Zamora as though that should have been obvious.

"To you," asks the curator unable to mask his surprise.

"Yes. The Richardsons left me the artifacts in their will with the stipulation that I carry out the original agreement that was drafted between them and your country. It has taken me two years to secure the support of my government, and the approval of your government to bring the artifacts to you."

"I see," states the curator in a voice that doesn't speak of understanding anything at all.

"Are you unwilling to agree to the terms agreed upon two years ago?"

"No," he begins, but at Zamora's raised eyebrow he stumbles around his words, "I mean, yes I am stilling willing to agree to the terms. I'm just a little surprised that they would want the artifacts returned to the states, especially in light of all that has occurred since their death."

More than a little curious as to what he means, Zamora states, "Well since they aren't, weren't aware of those events, it stands to reason that they wouldn't have made any other provisions for the art work other than the original provisions that they set up while still alive."

"Yes, yes. It does stand to reason," he states somewhat absently. However, he quickly recovers, "Once I sign the agreement, how soon will the artifacts arrive," he asks over anxiously. At least that's the way it appears to the three agents sitting in his office.

"From what I understand, it can take up to two weeks for the agreement to be bonded by your government and mine, but once that process is complete the artifacts should arrive with five days after that."

"Wonderful," he states as he signs his name on the dotted line, and Zamora does the same.

"I'm sure that I shall love visiting your country while we wait out the processing of the paper work," states Zamora as she places the agreement back in her sack and stands to leave.

"You're staying in the country," ask the curator in a very surprised tone.

"Of course," answers Zamora as though that was a strange question for him to ask. "I must make sure that the artifacts arrive safely, and be present for the authentication process as per the agreement."

"Yes, yes. Of course," responds Orogotto. He stands as he prepares to take them back down the long corridor to the museum foyer. Everyone is deep in thought as they walk the corridor, so silence surrounds them. Once at the foyer, Orogotto says, "Please enjoy your stay in my country, and if you need anything while you're here, please call my office. I will provide whatever assistance I am able."

"Thank you Monsieur Orogotto. I will keep that in mind," responds Zamora as cordially as she possibly can with the hairs standing up on the back of her neck.

New Developments

As soon as they are securely within the confines of the limo, Zamora studies Erik and Marquise to see if they developed the same uneasy feeling that she did while in the curators office. After only a few moments, she assesses that they did indeed get the same feeling she got. "So what are we going to do about it," she asks fully expecting them to understand what she was asking.

"Not sure," states Marquise. "But I intend to keep close tabs on the Monsieur," he continues, sarcastically saying the word monsieur. "By the way, who are the Richardsons too you?"

Zamora remains quiet for some time before responding in a far away voice, "My parents."

When she says no more, Erik jumps in, "Your parents?" She simply looks at him, but says no more. "That's all you're going to say?" She still remains quiet. "Isn't this case a little too personal for you to be working?"

"This case is quite personal," she all but growls at him, "but there wouldn't be a case if it wasn't for me so there is no way that I'm not seeing it through to the end." She remains quiet for just a few seconds before muttering somewhat under her breath, "Damn young'n wants to tell me, of all people, that the case is too personal for me to be working." Then she turns and glares at him until he puts his shades on his face and turns toward the window to observe the scenery as they drive back to the hotel.

"Czar, was that necessary," asks Marquise, his voice barely above a whisper. When she turns her glare his way, he simply grins at her with that sexy as hell grin of his. She finally gives up on the glare, and smiles back at him. "That's my girl," are his answering words.

Zamora tries to ignore the warm sensation that spreads through her at his words, however, both Marquise and Erik notice how her whole demeanor softened at his words. Erik wonders what is going on between his two fellow agents. He didn't think any of them had worked together before, but there is something tangible between these two. He decides he will just keep his eyes and ears open where they are concerned. Marquise finds that he must fight to maintain his control and not move over to her, and kiss her for all he's worth. They each decide there is too much tension building inside the limo, and turn to look out a window for the rest of the ride back to the hotel.

Once inside the comfort of their suite, they each head to their respective rooms to change into more casual clothing. Marquise is more concerned about Zamora than ever, and makes another call.

"Cockroach."

"Pathfinder here."

"Questions?"

"Monsieur Orogotto and his assistant."

"How deep?"

"Maximum depth. Will retrieve."

Heart Body and Soul

The line goes dead, and Marquise lies back on the bed trying to contemplate his next move in a case that appears to more complex than he originally suspected. "What has this woman gotten me into now," he asks himself. "Damn, talking to myself again."

Erik decides he needs some fresh air, and says as much to the closed doors of Zamora and Marquise as he leaves the suite. He makes his way to the outdoor market to see what goods are available and to clear his head. As he inspects some hand woven baskets, he hears a voice that sounds suspiciously like the voice of the woman from the museum.

"I'm telling you that it's her," the voice says.

"You don't know that," states the other voice.

"Who else would have the artifacts but the Princess now that the King and Queen have been taken care of? I wonder why it's taken her two years to bring them here."

"I still don't believe that couple that was killed was the King and Queen. They all died years ago on that airplane. These people probably bought the artifacts on the black market after someone found them in the wreckage from that plane."

"Don't believe it. I know it's her," states the young lady from the museum before storming away from the market.

Erik remains in the shadows, and is not seen by either of the women. He continues to inspect baskets for another ten minutes before moving to another stand that has hand woven cloths. After another twenty minutes at the market, he heads back to the hotel.

*****

Zamora removes her clothing and takes a shower after entering the confines of her room. As the water runs over her skin, she states out loud,

"That man is just too sexy for his own good." But she can't help but smile to herself as she remembers the look he gave her in the limo. After fifteen minutes under the cascading water she gets out, and walks into her room without benefit of a towel.

"My, my," drawls Marquise as his eyes roam over her body from head to toe.

Zamora nearly jumps out of her skin, and gives a yelp of surprise. "You scared the shit out of me," she nearly yells at him. "What are you doing in here?"

"I came in here to talk you about our visit at the museum, I just never suspected that you would come out of the bathroom as naked as the day you were born," he states in a somewhat teasing manner. "However, I would like to know how long you plan on torturing me for scaring you?"

"Oh, I haven't begun to torture you, but the thought has crossed my mind."

"Sweetheart you're torturing me just by standing there like that."

"Huh," says Zamora before getting a full glance at herself in the mirror attached to the dresser. As a result of her scare, she forgot that she was completely naked. "Shit," she growls as she makes her way back into the bathroom to retrieve her robe. She hears his laughter as she puts her arms through the sleeves. "This is not funny," she states as she walks back into her room.

"Yes it is. But seriously, I think we need to talk about these artifacts and how they came to be in your parent's possession."

"To be honest, I have no idea," she responds. "I mean as far back as I can remember they have been a part of our lives," she continues. "I can remember sitting on my father's lap at the age of five, and him explaining to me what each piece meant. Because they had been there from the beginning, I never thought to ask my parents where they originally came from," she concludes.

"Is it possible that they bought them on the black market?"

Zamora immediately becomes enraged and marches across the room to him, "There is no way my parents bought them off the black market," she growls at him while accentuating each word with a jab of her finger into his chest. "And I deeply resent you even suggesting that they did!"

When she is done with her tirade, Marquise grabs her hands to prevent further assault by her, "I think we need to find out how they acquired them as that information could be key to the case." He fights to hold on to her hands as her rage increases, "If they came by them legitimately, maybe the people they purchased them from came by them on the black market. It's a possibility that we must explore. That became painfully obvious by the way the curator reacted to the fact that the artifacts are to be returned to you once the terms of the agreement have been met."

Knowing that he is right, Zamora loses some of her steam and relaxes just a little, "I know that you're right, however, no one wants to think ill of their parents especially when those parents aren't around to defend themselves."

"I know Sweetheart," he responds while giving her the hug he feels she so desperately needs right now. "Are there papers outlining the purchase of the artifacts?

"No there aren't," responds Zamora. "I believe that they were passed down to my parents by a family member."

"What family member?"

"I think it was a great-aunt on my father's side, but I can't be sure."

"Okay, we'll come back to that later. Where are the authentication papers associated with artifacts?"

59

"Rock has them at the compound for safe keeping until the artifacts arrive."

"Then I think we need to pay Rock a visit and fully investigate the papers. Now get dressed," he states while giving her behind a quick smack. At her glare he walks out of the room laughing.

Heart Body and Soul

Updates

Just as Marquise takes a seat in the common area to wait for Zamora to emerge fully dressed, in walks Erik, "Can I have a word with you," Erik asks Marquise.

"Sure man, what's up?"

"I overheard the woman from the museum and another woman talking in the market place. The woman from the museum is completely convinced that Zamora is this missing Princess, and I believe she is planning on letting the people who killed her parents know that she is here and that the artifacts are soon to arrive. I think we are going to need a plan that Zamora doesn't know about on the outside chance that these people try to kidnap her, or just outright kill her."

"I agree Erik," begins Marquise, "and after we meet with Rock and verify the authenticity of the papers associated with artifacts, we'll be better able to chart a course of action. Once we return from the compound and she has gone to bed tonight, we will devise a plan to save her life and find out who's behind all of this."

"Great. When are we leaving?"

"Just as soon as Czar joins us. She's getting dressed."

As if on cue, the door to Zamora's room opens and she emerges. "Ready to go boys?"

"Yes," they say in unison, and the trio heads over to the FBI compound for a debriefing of the day's events.

Once outside of the city limits, the trio stops at a little village to change into different clothes, as well as, switch vehicles. They don't need anyone putting two and two together and figuring out that they are agents posing as art curators.

When they arrive at the compound, they head straight for the conference room to update Rock on everything that has taken place since they left the compound a couple of days before.

"So, some people think that you are the missing Princess," Rock asks Zamora.

"Yes, and isn't that more than strange since I have been here before and no one thought that I was her?"

"Maybe it's the artifacts that make them think that you are her. From what I understand, the royal family would have never parted with them even in death. So, relate to me again how your parents gained possession of them?"

"I really don't know how they came to be in my parent's possession. I remember the artifacts being part of our home for all of my life. It never occurred to me to ask where they came from, and when my parents said that they were bringing the artifacts back here to Africa because that was where they truly belonged, I didn't question them then either. It was their art work to do whatever they chose to do with it."

"Well it would help us out considerably if you knew how they acquired the art," responds Rock.

"I can check through their papers, and see if I can find out how they came to own them. Although, I don't recall seeing anything about their purchase when I put their estate in order after their death. I think my father inherited them from a relative, but since all my immediate relatives are all deceased I have no one to ask. I know I didn't see anything in my Nana's papers after her death," replies Zamora. She then goes on to add, "I guess we'll just have to protect them as best we can while we wait to have their authenticity verified at the museum."

"I guess we will, but in the meantime I want you to try to blend in as much as possible. We don't need anyone accidently interfering in our investigation because they are trying to figure out if you are the long lost princess of this kingdom," states Rock.

Zamora heads to the small conference room to go through her parent's papers. She is grateful that she had them shipped over just in case she needed to find something in them while working the case.

The men use this opportunity to talk about the new developments in the case. "Tell me again about the people that thought that Czar was their missing princess," states Rock.

"As we were walking through the airport, an elderly gentleman dropped to his knees and declared her the princess, and told her to be careful," begins Marquise. "He even told her to go underground before she met the same fate as her parents."

"Then there were the market women who also dropped to their knees, and began crying while declaring her the missing princess," adds Erik. "She is now wearing a shroud while out in public to keep others from seeing too much of her face, so that we don't have a repeat of the events that took place at the airport."

"That's good. I'll have to have someone look into this missing royal family, and see if there is any connection to Zamora or her parents," states Rock. "I never concerned myself with her lack of family before, but now it's nagging at me," he continues. "I will let you know as soon as I have some answers," he concludes.

"I can give you a starting point," states Marquise and all eyes turn his way. "After the two incidents at the airport, I did some digging once we got to the hotel," he begins. "King Zuriel and Queen Zawadi Umboto where being harassed by King Gamboto to marry off their daughter to one of his sons so that the two kingdoms could be combined. However, the Umbotos would not agree to the marriage and the Gamboto Kingdom launched a full-fledged assault against the Umboto Kingdom, including trying to kidnap the princess," he continues. "I suspect that the Umbotos knew that the Gambotos wanted control of their diamond mines, and that they would treat their people unjustly," he states. "The Umbotos fled the country with their daughter, and apparently the royal family artwork, however, it was believed that they all perished in a plane crash over the ocean. Apparently the royal family did not trust a lot of people, and rightly so, so they boarded the plane with a village infant. The true Princess and the royal artifacts were smuggled out of the country by servants, and no one in this country had heard another word about them or the artifacts until Czar's parent's brought news of the artifacts here two years ago," he concludes.

"What was the princess's name," asks Rock.

"Zahara," answers Marquise.

"I'm not going to ask how you came across all this information, but good work," states Rock as Erik looks on amazed but grateful that he has more information to use in his own investigation.

"I know I'm new to this, but there is a lot more going on here than we suspect," begins Erik. "Czar doesn't know that I overheard the greeter from the museum taking to another woman in the market place, and they seem to be affiliated with or at least know the people that killed her parents. The woman from the museum is convinced that her parents were the King and Queen, and that she is the Princess. I believe that her life is in real danger, and that we need a new plan to keep her alive. One that she doesn't know about."

64

"I totally agree," adds Marquise. "I'm thinking that this is going to get a lot more complicated than we originally anticipated."

"In the meantime, let's take a look at the US papers authenticating the artifacts," states Rock.

Authenticity

Rock retrieves the papers from the safe that were given to him by the National Museum of African Art. The documents outline the materials used to create the artifacts, as well as, the tools used to create the intricate carvings and detailed designs found on the pieces of artwork. It is evident from all of the processes employed that the artifacts were indeed created in Africa, and are truly authentic.

Along with the details of each piece of artwork, there is a document outlining the history of each piece of art. There is no evidence that the artwork was stolen from its rightful owners, and sold on the black market. Although it is documented that the artwork was originally commissioned by the first King and Queen of Umboto and passed down to each successive King and Queen, there is no documentation on how it came to be in the possession of the Richardsons.

Puzzled by the missing information, Rock makes a few phone calls stateside to determine why the papers on rightful ownership are missing from the papers he was given. He is frustrated immensely as he is not able to get a definitive answer from anyone that he speaks to, and is told that the matter will have to be investigated which could take days or even weeks before a reasonable explanation is received.

"The King and Queen were defecting to the US for Asylum when they were killed, correct," asks Marquise.

"That is correct," answers Rock. "Why?"

"What if they weren't killed? What if the Richardsons were indeed the King and Queen, and somehow managed to place someone else on the plane that crashed? What if they successfully made it to America, and in an effort to protect them we gave them new identities? And in order to protect their new identities, the rightful ownership papers were intentionally left out of the documentation?"

"That's a lot of what ifs Marquise," responds Rock.

Marquise rubs his hand down his face in frustration, "I know. I know. I'm just trying to make sense of all of this." He begins pacing, "There are just too many missing pieces of information, and I don't like it."

"When the Richardsons first approach the State Department about bringing the artifacts back to this country there was a lot of opposition from the powers that be, then in the bat of an eye they were being given full clearance to come to this country and negotiate with the government here and the IFAN Museum," states Rock.

"Who was responsible for the change of heart," asks Erik.

"To be honest, I don't remember, but I can certainly find out." With that being said, Rock makes a few more phone calls stateside.

When Rock rejoins them, he has a deep crease in his forehead that does not sit well with Marquise. "What did you learn that you don't like?"

"What makes you think that I don't like what I've learned?"

"The deep furrow in the middle of your forehead."

Rock attempts to relax his facial features before responding, "You're quite correct. I don't like what I've just heard. It seems that E-Dub's great-grandparents had a lot to do with the Richardsons being granted permission to return the artifacts to African, and were the ones to suggest that they merely be loaned to IFAN."

"Why does that bother you," asks Erik.

"Because E-Dub never mentioned that he knew of Zamora, or her parents, or the artifacts. I think it strange that their paths never crossed if his great-grandparents were close enough to the Richardson's to go to bat for them on something of this magnitude."

"That is more that passing strange," admits Marquise as he muses over what Rock has just revealed.

"Does E-Dub have a close relationship with his great-grandparents," asks Erik at the lull in the conversation.

"Very close, from what I've been told," answers Rock. "That's why it's bothering me that he never crossed paths with the Richardsons."

"What if he has crossed paths with them, and is withholding that information on purpose? What if he has some other agenda for being on this mission?"

"What is with you and the what ifs," Erik asks of Marquise.

"It's a way to explore all possibilities, and rule out the ones that are highly unlikely," Marquise responds somewhat absent mindedly. "What was the nature of the relationship between the senior Whittmores and the Richardsons?"

"From what I learned, the Whittmores were instrumental in helping the Richardsons become acclimated to life in Washington Politics when they joined the staff at the Smithsonian as African Historians."

"They weren't from Africa, how could they be considered African Historians," asks a confused Erik.

"Apparently they were American relatives of an African Family with a long history in Africa. The stories they told were able to be validated by African Studies programs all over the world, not to mention that the artifacts that they possessed were declared authentic. They were able to validate truths of African history, as well as, dispose of untruths."

"This is all sounding as though Zamora might be in more danger than we thought if someone on this continent believes she has direct ties to the land here, and is trying to gain control of that land," states Erik.

"I agree with you E&J," responds Rock.

New Plan

"So what are we going to do to keep her safe," asks Marquise.

"I am going to give you some cameras to hide in her clothing that will allow us to have a 360 degree look at her surroundings whenever she leaves the hotel," states Rock. "How you will be able to get them in her clothing without her knowing is something you will have to figure out for yourselves, but at least we will be able to monitor everyone that is monitoring her," he adds.

"I can get the job done with no problem," states Marquise. "I am already familiar with the cameras if they are the same ones that we used in the Seals," he adds. "So that she doesn't ask what we have, I suggest you have them delivered to the suite before we return," he further adds.

"I agree," responds Rock as he walks over to his desk to have everything they will need delivered while the trio is still at the compound.

"Will there be a hand-held monitor included," asks Marquise as soon as Rock gets off the phone.

"Yes," is Rock's response.

"Can someone let me know what is going on," asks Erik.

"I'll explain everything to you as soon as Zamora goes to sleep tonight," states Marquise.

"Great," says Erik while rolling his eyes.

"You'll be brought up to speed, young'n," quips Marquise while grinning from ear to ear.

Shortly thereafter, Zamora enters the main room looking none too pleased. "I have found nothing about the artifacts in all their papers," she states dejectedly. "But there are two more boxes to go through, however, I don't think we should stay gone too much longer else the natives might become suspicious."

"I agree," states Marquise. "When we debrief in a couple of days, you can go through more of the papers then."

"Be safe you three," states Rock as they head towards the compound exit.

When the three of them finally make it back to the hotel, Zamora goes to her room to be alone to think and Erik and Marquise go to his room to look at the equipment that Rock sent over. As they unpack everything, Marquise explains to Erik how each piece works.

"These are the cameras and they are equipped with mics so we can see as well as hear," he states as he holds up something that resembles a small hearing aid battery but that is as light as a plastic button. "This is the handheld console that we can use to monitor the cameras and mics," he adds as he holds up a device that resembles a cellular phone.

"How are we supposed to get the cameras in Zamora's clothing without her knowing about it," asks Erik.

"Leave that to me," states Marquise. At the raising of Erik's eyebrows, Marquise continues, "I knew Zamora before I was an agent. Hell before I knew she was an agent. And I had no idea that we would be on this case together, and neither did she. As a matter of fact until she arrived here in Africa, we hadn't seen each other for two years."

"So are you two rekindling an old romance?"

"To be honest, I don't know what we are doing. We didn't exactly have a real relationship before." They are both quiet for a few moments before Marquise says, "Don't worry about it, Zamora and I can handle being together and it not interfere with the case."

Erik holds up his hands, "I'm not saying anything man. You two are the senior agents here, I'm still learning the ropes."

"Let me show how the handheld works just in case I'm not able to do the monitoring." The two of them spend the next hour going through all the capabilities of the surveillance equipment before Erik leaves Marquise's room to do some research of his own.

Marquise contacts Cockroach to see if he has retrieved the information he asked him for.

"Cockroach."

"Pathfinder here."

"First let me say, be careful my friend, as you seem to be headed into an anaconda birthing pit."

"Damn! Care to tell me who's all following the lady's scent?"

"You already know the Gambotos want the artifacts, however, there is an unknown American on her tail as well, not to mention Orogotto who doesn't want to return the artifacts to her as the agreement states. Apparently he is a descendent of a past king of the Umboto tribe, but was banished for some slight against the kingdom. He believes that he can rightfully claim the throne if he has the artifacts. Not sure if he believes

Czar to be the princess or not. He probably doesn't care since he's plotting with the Gambotos to have her killed, who have pledged to help in exchange for Orogotto marrying one of their daughters and merging the two kingdoms. However, I think that the Gambotos are planning to get rid of Orogotto after the marriage, and claim the kingdom outright."

"Damn!!! Who's the American? And why is he on her tail?"

"He is a man of mystery as no one can identify him, however, he is believed to be a black market art dealer. Any successful black market stings that have take place in the last ten years have one thing in common, an unknown American. And each group of thieves describes him differently, so no one is sure if it's the same person in disguise or multiple people. I was unable to determine who he plans to sell the artifacts to once he gets his hands on them, but there are reports of an American speaking with both Orogotto and the Gambotos. He just may be plotting against both his buyers to get the best deal for himself."

"Shit! This is getting infinitely more complicated that I could have ever imagined! Thanks for the info."

"I'm a stone's throw away when you need me."

"Thanks."

The line is disconnected, and Marquise is left pacing as he tries to navigate this latest turn in the mission he was sent here to complete. After an hour of pacing and thinking and a hot shower, Marquise sets his mind to getting the cameras hidden in Zamora's clothes. "We need these more so now than we did three hours ago," he says to himself while putting the cameras in his pants pocket before heading to Zamora's room.

Alternate Agenda

Once the trio leaves the compound, Rock starts exploring E-Dub's background and history with the agency. What he didn't let the others know is that, the Elder Whittmores appear to have close ties to the Gamboto tribe as they have negotiated deals on their behalf with the American Government in the past.

Rock starts reviewing the nature of those negotiations, and becomes more than a little suspicious of the connection that the Elder Whittmores have with the Gambotos. He continues digging into their past, and learns that they are direct descendents of the tribe. Apparently the elder Mr. Whittmore is the grandson of a lesser prince of the tribe who was cast out for trying to kill his older brother who was next in line for the throne. He moved to America and changed his name to Rashad Whittmore, and never returned to his country. He eventually married Selena Rodriquez, and they had three sons, Enrique Sr., Juan, and Alejandro. Enrique Sr. married Alessa Gonzales at the age of 28, and their marriage only produced one child, Enrique Jr. Enrique Jr. had fallen in love with and had an affair with the daughter of a visiting Spanish dignitary, and she gave birth to E-Dub. Her parents believed that Enrique was not good enough for their daughter, and forbid them to be together. Once she gave birth to her child, her parents sent the child back to America to be raised by its father. However, Enrique Jr. was reminded daily of the love he had for his son's mother every time he looked in his face, and traveled to Spain to steal the woman of his heart. They were both killed trying to leave the country, leaving their only child an orphan who was then raised by his grandparents and great-grandparents. Trying to compensate for the loss of his parents, they spoiled him rotten.

E-Dub learned of the tragedy that befell his parents at the age of 16, and became extremely unruly to the point that his grandparents enrolled him in military school to keep him from wrecking havoc on the world. The military seemed to give him purpose, and he continued serving in the military until he joined the agency at age 40. In the ten years he's been with the agency, there are a few question marks on his service record however nothing was ever proven. Then Rock sees something that makes the hairs stand up on the back of his neck, it is believed that E-Dub was in Africa two years ago when the Richardsons died. However, the evidence wasn't conclusive as E-Dub's alibi couldn't be disproven nor could it be proven with certainty either. Rock decides to dig deeper into the question marks in E-Dub's file.

"I swear if he has an alternate agenda that will cause Czar harm, he will rue the day he joined my team," states Rock. "I can't afford to have M&M and E&J thinking that they can't trust him, so I'm going to have to form an alternate agenda of my own."

With that thought firmly planted in his mind, Rock places a few phones calls to call in some favors he's owed.

"Cockroach."

"Blackjack."

"False Shuffle?"

"Looking for a shill."

"Suspect?"

"Sidewinder."

A long drawn out breath is released followed by a long silence before a response is given. "Two clicks." And the line goes dead.

Rock leans back in his chair for he knows that Cockroach and Sidewinder have had run ins in the past, and Cockroach has been waiting on an opportunity to take him down. However, he knows that Cockroach will only do so on legitimate information. "This is not what I signed up for when I agreed to come over here," states Rock to the empty office. "I came here to bust some black market art dealers, not save the life of an unknown princess or bring in a rogue agent." He runs his hand over his head as he ponders how to keep M&M and E&J from finding out about E-Dub while letting them know they may have to protect her from yet another possible assassin.

*****

The sound of his cell phone beeping two hours later brings Rock out of his musings about the assignment he currently finds himself on.

"Blackjack."

"Cockroach."

"Verdict?"

"Links to several black market deals, however, not solid enough to charge him with the crimes. He does have a connection to a movie studio make-up artist that could be the reason he has a different look on every deal he's been linked to, and I believe I've found some offshore accounts that he's been stock piling money into. At least the accounts are linked to the face of the Americans believed to be involved with each one of the black market deals. Also, those same faces have been identified as being seen at each one of Sidewinder's alibi locations. Don't think it's a coincidence."

"Shit! I'll need those photos."

"On their way."

"May need an extra deck."

"On hand if you need me."

They disconnect the call just as there is a knock on Rock's office door, and then an envelope is slid underneath it. Figuring it's the photos from Cockroach, Rocks walks over and picks up the envelope. Sure enough it's the pictures of the unknown Americans. Rock scans in the photos, and then sends them to M&M and E&J's phones with a message to keep an eye out for any of the Americans in the photos.

*****

E&J is still in the downstairs lounge of the hotel when the photos hit his phone. "Shit," he whispers upon seeing the message. "Like we need another twist in this plot."

Seduction for a Cause

Marquise quietly knocks on Zamora's door. He doesn't get a response, so he opens the door and walks in. He finds Zamora sitting in the middle of the bed surrounded by cassette tapes, and wearing headphones. Then she begins to frantically write in a notepad that he did not notice sitting in her lap. He watches her unobserved for fifteen minutes before he decides to walk over to the bed to get her attention.

She nearly jumps off the bed as the sound he makes scares her half to death. She stops the cassette player and snatches the headphones off her ears, "What the hell happened to knocking," she yells at him.

Surprised by her reaction, he fights to maintain an even tone in his voice as he responds, "I did knock, you didn't answer so I opened the door to check on you and saw you sitting there listening to whatever those tapes are," he begins. "As a matter of fact, I've been standing here for over fifteen minutes but you were so engrossed in those tapes that you didn't even notice my presence," he concludes.

"Well if you did knock and I didn't respond, what made you think I wasn't sleeping or just didn't want to be bothered," she asks with anger still in her voice.

"Whoa," states Marquise as he holds his hands up in surrender, "Where the hell is all the anger coming from? I didn't think you would get this upset about me coming in here or I wouldn't have dared," he states getting angry himself.

"Well, I'm trying to have a private moment, and I don't need your interference," she states as she gathers up the tapes and begins placing them in her shoulder bag.

Marquise more than curious about the tapes, walks over to the bed and picks one up. The writing on the label is in French, the primary language spoken in Dakar. Not overly fluent in French, he is not able to decipher most of the writing but he does recognize the names of the missing royal family. "What are these? And where did you get them," he asks with anger still in his voice.

Zamora snatches the tape from his hand while stating, "None of your business."

Marquise grabs her by the arms and lifts her off the bed, "I'm going to ask you one more time, what are these tapes and where did you get them?"

Nose to nose with him Zamora is slightly intimidated but refuses to back down, "I don't have to tell you damn thing," she states defiantly.

Turned on by the anger flashing in her eyes and the sound of it in her voice, Marquise gives her a punishing kiss which quickly turns heated on both of their parts. The anger leaves the kiss and the passion between them quickly flares. He lets go of her arms to cup the back of her neck and wrap an arm around her waist so that he can deepen the kiss. Unable to resist, Zamora wraps her arms around his neck and accepts every ounce of passion he is placing into the kiss. Before either one of them know it, they are both naked and making love as though their lives depended on it. In no time at all they both reach completion, and are lying in each other's arms desperately trying to pull air into their lungs and slow the rapid beating of their hearts.

Once he is able to talk, Marquise asks, "What just happened here?"

"To be honest, I'm not sure," begins Zamora. "You caught me off guard, and I took my anger and frustration at my parents out on you," she continues. "I really didn't mean for all of this to happen, and this is not how I envisioned this case going," she adds. "My parents obviously had some really big secrets that they were keeping from me, and I'm not sure what to do with what I'm feeling."

"Okay, I'm more confused now than ever. Care to elaborate on what you just said?"

"I found the tapes in my parent's papers. The tapes apparently were made by the King and Queen of Umboto, and they detail all the events that lead up to their departure from their kingdom. However, the truly confusing part is the tapes that were made after they were supposed to have died in the plane crash. I don't believe I have ever met these people, but it seems as though my parents were really close to them. They may even have been related, and I'm not sure how I feel about that."

"Do you believe that there is any truth to the belief that your parents are/were the missing King and Queen of this country? And that you are the missing Princess?"

"While there seems to be a lot of coincidences in our lives, I believe that my parents would have told me about this if it were true. Especially if they knew there was a chance they could be harmed by coming back to this country. No, I don't believe that we are this missing royal family."

"Can I ask you to do me a favor?"

"I suppose."

"Consider the possibility that you are this Princess, and that there are still people in this country that either want you dead, or married off to this Gamboto Prince and then disposed of. It just might save your life while we're here."

Heart Body and Soul

She suddenly gives in to all the conflicting emotions inside of her, and tears begin to roll down her face. Marquise leans over to kiss the moisture from her cheeks, and as he nears her lips she turns her head so that his next kiss lands there. She snakes out her tongue and licks his lips. He quickly pulls her tongue into his mouth, and the passion between them flares to life. When the need to breathe becomes too strong to ignore, Marquise releases her mouth and trails kisses across her cheek to her neck then on to her breasts. Here he stops to pull a budding nipple into his mouth to suckle. Zamora moans loudly at the sensations his mouth is creating inside of her as he feasts on her breasts, and this only increases the adrenaline flowing through Marquise's body. He makes his way down her flat stomach, stopping only long enough to dip his tongue into her navel, before venturing lower to that part of her that makes her woman. Needing the full taste of her in his mouth, he sinks his tongue deep inside of her. Their joint moans mingle together as he savors her taste and she is overwhelmed by the way he is loving her with his mouth. He makes love to her this way until she screams his name in the midst of a giant orgasm. He removes his mouth from her woman's mound only after the last tremble leaves her body, and then enters her in one swift thrust. The sensation of being buried to the hilt inside of her nearly does him in, so he remains motionless for quite some time as he tries to regain control of his senses. Realizing what is happening and not wanting it to be over too quickly, Zamora remains motionless as well.

Once he feels that he is in control of his body once again, he pulls almost completely out of her only to slowly bury himself inside of her once again. He keeps up this slow pace until Zamora can't stand it and whispers in his ear, "Don't play with me, take me. Now."

Her words are his undoing, and he gives her the hard deep thrusts she's craving. Her moans of ecstasy add fuel to the fire, and his pace increases until she's screaming his name as another orgasm rips through her. However, he's not ready for the loving to end, so he slows his pace to prime her for another explosive round of love making. After her fourth orgasm, he's more than ready to find completion himself and whispers in her ear, "One more baby. Give me one more and I'll join you this time."

His words are all the encouragement she needs to wrap her legs around his waist holding him tightly to her as he continues to work his shaft in and out of her love cove. Twenty minutes later they are both screaming out their joy as an orgasm of gigantic proportions sweeps through both of them. They lay there in each other's arms trying desperately to pull much needed oxygen into their lungs, and before he knows it Zamora is fast asleep.

He disengages himself from her legs and arms, and covers her with the sheets from the bed. Not wanting to make too much noise, he takes all of her shrouds and few other items of clothing from her room to his room to install the cameras. On the off chance that she ventures out without one of the head coverings, he also installs a few into a few of her blouses. Once his work is complete, he replaces all of her clothing without her knowing a thing. Knowing that she will not think it strange that he is not there when she wakes up, he heads back to his room for some much needed rest.

As he enters the sitting area, he notices Erik sitting in one of the chairs watching TV. "Did you get the job done," asks Erik. Marquise tilts his head to one side as he ponders Erik's question. "I know you got the job done since I walked in here in the midst of a whole lot of moaning and screaming. What I would like to know is did you get the cameras installed?"

"Funny," replies Marquise, before adding, "Not." He then continues on at Erik's silence, "Yes, I got the job done, and I am referring to the cameras." Seeing that Erik is struggling not to laugh, he states, "I'm going to take a nap."

"Before your nap, check your phone," states E&J.

"Why?"

"Rock sent us some photos of Americans that have been linked to black market art deals, and he wants us to keep an eye out for them in the village."

82

Heart Body and Soul

"Shit, like we need more players on the field," states Marquise before entering his room.

Playing the Players

The following morning they receive a message from Monsieur Orogotto to meet him at the museum as he has an urgent matter to discuss with Zariah/Zamora. Unsure as to what the urgent matter could be, the trio wastes no time getting dressed and heading to the museum. Once they arrive the same young lady is there to greet them, and she is intensely studying Zamora the whole time they wait for the curator to emerge from his office.

When he reaches the atrium, he instructs them to follow him to his office before heading back in that direction at a fast pace. Once they are inside his office, he introduces them to a gentleman who has a very smug look on his face. "Femme Robinson meet Enrique White, a specialist in African Artifacts from the US," he states to Zamora before turning back to the gentleman, "This is Femme Robinson and her associates Erik Jackson and Marquise Markinson."

"I wish I could say that it is a pleasure to meet you Mademoiselle, however, under the circumstances it's not," states Mr. White. Marquise and Erik go on instant alert so as not to alert the Monsieur that E-Dub is merely playing a role.

Fighting hard to maintain her composure since E-Dub seems to be enjoying being as rude as possible to her, Zamora simply turns her attention to the curator, "Monsieur, what is the meaning of this," she asks.

Heart Body and Soul

Without giving the man a chance to answer, she fires more questions at him, "Exactly who is this gentleman? What is he doing here? And what does this have to do with me?"

"I am here to expose you as the fraud that you are," the gentleman responds before the curator could say a word. "You did not know the Richardsons, and there is no way that you can possess the artifacts that they had in their possession prior to their death," he continues. "I knew them rather well, and there is no way that they would have left that art work to you," he concludes.

"Apparently you didn't know them as well as you think you do since they indeed did leave the artifacts to me in their will," responds Zamora heatedly. "I have no idea what fabrications you have told the Monsieur, but I am confident that you will be exposed as a fraud once the artifacts arrive and the Monsieur is able to inspect them." She then turns to the Monsieur, "I'm not sure what is going on here, but I assure you that my government would not have made it possible for me to come here if I was a fraud," she begins. "And quite frankly I'm insulted that you would summon me here for this man to defame me in such a manner," she continues. As she turns towards the door, she says over her shoulder, "I'm sure my government would love to know how rudely I was just treated." Not waiting for Marquise and Erik to join her, she walks through the door and down the long hallway to the atrium.

Marquise pulls the handheld from his pocket and turns it on. With its size and shape resembling a cell phone, no one in the room is the wiser about what he is up to. In the meantime, Erik turns to the curator and the unknown gentlemen, "I assure you that Femme Robinson is not a fraud. I have seen the artifacts and the paperwork surrounding how they came to be in Zariah's possession, and I assure you that they are genuine." He then too turns and walks out the door to join Zamora.

Not overly concerned about the events that just took place, Marquise turns to both men and says, "Good day gentlemen," before joining the others in the limo for the ride back to the hotel. The ride back is a silent one as they do not want to alert anyone that what just took place at the museum was all a ruse. They all know that they will debrief once inside their suite.

Once inside the room, Marquise is the first to speak, "Very nice performance back there," he states to Zamora.

She bows while saying, "Thank you. You are too kind sir." Marquise and Erik simply shake their heads at her before they all burst into a fit of laughter. Once they are over there amusement with the situation, Zamora asks, "I wonder what moves the Monsieur made after everyone left?"

"I'm sure E-Dub will tell us at the next debriefing," replies Marquise. He then asks Zamora, "What were your plans for the day since we weren't scheduled to do much today?"

"I was actually going to explore the local market place today. Try to see if I could overhear any conversations by the natives to see if anyone is speculating on the missing princess or the artifacts."

"Good idea," states Erik, "Mind if I tag along?"

"Not at all," she replies. "Would you like to join us as well?"

"Don't mind if I do," is Marquise's response.

The trio leaves the suite to explore the market place with Marquise frequently monitoring the handheld device to see who is interested in their movements. Unbeknownst to them, Giovanni is making his move as the US Ambassador sent to oversee the transition of the artifacts from America to Africa, as well as, see who's who in the black market.

"I am Giovanni Lawson, US Ambassador to Dakar, and I am here to see Monsieur Orogotto," states GL as he reaches the young lady set up to greet visitors to IFAN.

Heart Body and Soul

"The Monsieur only receives visitors by appointment," she states in a somewhat abrasive voice as though she is unconcerned about the title that he gave after his name.

"I beg your pardon," responds GL.

"You can beg all you like, you still will not be meeting the Monsieur," comes her flippant response.

"We'll see about that," states an angry GL. He immediately pulls out his cell phone, and makes a call.

In less than a minute after he ends his call, the Monsieur comes racing down the hall in his direction. "Please forgive my assistant," he states as he tries to catch his breath, "she takes herself a little too seriously at times," he adds while glowering at her. He then turns back to GL, "This way Ambassador Lawson. We can meet in my office."

Once they are inside the office, Orogotto takes his seat behind his desk as GL sits in a chair directly in front of the desk. "To what do I owe this surprise visit," Orogotto asks GL.

"I have come to warn you that a gentleman from my country is on his way to this country to try to put a wrinkle in the deal over the artifacts that Ms Robinson has so graciously agreed to let be displayed here," he begins. "I am here to inform you that Enrique White is a fraud, and only looking out for himself. He would like to keep the artifacts in America so that he may have a chance to steal them and sell them to the highest bidder on the black market," he continues. "I personally believe that he has been in touch with the Gamboto Kingdom, and plans to give them first option on purchasing the artifacts so that they may gain control of the Umboto Kingdom," he concludes while closely studying the curator. He notices the slight clenching of the curators jaw and the slight twitching of his right eye as the curator processes the information that he has just given to him.

"It seems your warning is a little late for Monsieur White was here this morning, and I summoned your Femme Robinson here to hear his claim that she was a fraud," replies Orogotto. "She was quite upset when she left here after hearing his accusations," he adds quietly.

"I'm sure she was," responds GL.

"She said that she would be contacting her government about the matter, and I assumed that that was the reason for your visit," states Orogotto. "I do not wish to lose the artifacts again because of this misunderstanding," he continues. "But the man had quite a bit of paperwork on the Femme that made me believe that his words were truth."

"All fraudulent, I assure you," states GL.

"Well this certainly causes me concern," replies Orogotto. "Can you please assure the Femme that I am still interested in the artifacts, and would like to honor our contract," he asks unable to disguise the desperation in his voice.

"I will do what I can to make sure that the contract is fulfilled, as this deal will go a long way in improving the relationship between your government and mine," responds GL.

Both gentlemen stand and extend their hands at the same time. "Thank you so much for taking the time to inform me about the motives of Monsieur White," states Orogotto.

"Like I said, it is in the best interest of both our countries that the contract on the artifacts is fulfilled," states GL.

Monsieur Orogotto escorts GL back to the atrium where they find it empty of the young lady who's supposed to greet all guests into the museum.

"I wonder where Sareena has gone to," comments Orogotto somewhat under his breath as GL walks out the door.

"So do I, so do I," states GL as he steps out the door.

Heart Body and Soul

Avoiding the Mongoose

As soon as GL has left the museum, Orogotto practically runs back to his office to place a call to Mr. White.

After several rings the phone is finally answered, "Mr. White, may I help you?"

"This is Monsieur Orogotto from IFAN."

"Greetings Monsieur Orogotto. I take it this phone call means that you believe me and not the tyrannical ramblings of that American woman."

"No sir it does not," begins Orogotto. "Your country's ambassador came by to see me after all of you left the museum. He states that you are a fraud, and under investigation by your government. He threatened to not let the artifacts be housed at the museum. I cannot let that happen, so Monsieur I would appreciate it if you did not stop by the museum again. Good Day." Orogotto promptly hangs up the phone.

"That sounded very convincing to anyone listening in on the museum's line," states E-Dub. "I still think the man is a rat, and doesn't plan to hold up his end of the deal. Time to make some moves of my own if this mission is going to be a success."

With that being said, he dons a disguise and sneaks out his hotel room through a back door. "Time to see what's happening in the Gamboto kingdom," he states as he emerges into the marketplace undetected as he is dressed in native garb. He rents a camel for his trip, and heads out to the Gamboto's palace.

Just as he arrives, he sees GL saying good-bye to the King and Queen. He is grateful to be in disguise for he had no prior knowledge of GL's trip to the kingdom nor is he supposed to be there himself. That could have proven quite awkward for both of them, however, it leaves him to wonder if GL's visit was sanctioned by Rock. And if it was, why wasn't he informed about it? He makes a mental note to delve into GL background a little more for if there is some under the table dealing going on, he damn sure will find out about it.

The skin on the back of GL's neck stands up at the approach of a loan rider on a camel, which is puzzling to him as he does not recognize the man. He doesn't believe that the King would allow a hired assassin to show up at the palace, since he is there to ensure that the Gambotos will not cause an international incident by trying to steal the Umboto artifacts once they arrive in this country. However, there is something familiar and unsettling about the man on the camel. Since he is unable to reconcile any of this in his mind, he climbs in the back of his vehicle and instructs his driver to take him back to his hotel.

"Your Majesties," states E-Dub while bowing before the King and Queen after dismounting from the camel, "is it possible to have a private word with you?"

"Just what would we be discussing," asks the King.

"The Umboto artifacts."

Both the King and Queen look at each and frown before turning back to the gentleman kneeling before them. "Follow us inside," states the King as he and the Queen turn and head back inside the palace.

Heart Body and Soul

Once inside their private chambers, the King asks the gentleman, "What could you possibly have to discuss about the Umboto artifacts?"

"What if I told you that I could get them for you?"

"Everyone around the world would know that they were stolen, and not rightfully ours. That would bring great scandal to my kingdom, and that, dear sir, I am not interested I doing."

"What if I said, I could produce paperwork that states the young lady who has them now stole them and that the rightful owners, who are now deceased, left them to this country upon their death?"

"That would still bring a lot of scrutiny to my kingdom that we can ill-afford. The gentleman leaving as you arrived is the US Ambassador to this country, and he has assured me that if the US detects any type of foul play in connection with my kingdom and the artifacts that his country would deal harshly with my kingdom. So, I am not interested in any deals you wish to make concerning the artifacts. Have a good day sir," states the King as he nods to a servant to come see the gentleman out of the palace and back to his camel.

As E-Dub enters the dessert, he says to himself, "Well played King. I hope you are sincere in stating that you do not wish to come by the artifacts illegally, for if we find out otherwise, well let's just say it wouldn't bode well for the Kingdom of Gamboto."

*****

"There was something unsettling about that man," states the Queen once she and the King are all alone.

"You felt it too," asks the King.

"Yes, I did. And I will be glad when we see the last of him."

"I agree," states the King. "Now about this US Ambassador," he states after a short pause, "what do you make of his visit?"

"I think he was on a hunting trip," responds the Queen. "He wanted to gauge our reaction to the threat of invasion by his government if anything happens to the artifacts. Unfortunately for him, he doesn't know how well trained we are not to show emotion in public. I don't think he is any wiser about us than he was before he arrived. It takes quite a cleaver mongoose to catch a snake, and I don't think he was that cleaver."

"Very well my dear," states the King. "Care to join me for an afternoon nap," asks the King with mischief in his eyes.

"I am feeling a bit tired after our visitors," states the Queen behind a fake yawn.

Third Eye Vision

As Zamora visits various stands at the market, Marquise hangs back periodically checking the handheld to see who is interested in her movements. For the first half hour it seems as though no one is interested in her, and then as she looks at some handmade cloth at a booth near the end of the market, he notices the greeter from the museum peeking at her from the side of a stall directly behind Zamora. He notices that she keeps talking over her shoulder to someone, and he wishes that Zamora would change her position so that he could get a better view of who she is talking to. His wish is granted a few minutes later as the other person peeks over the young lady's shoulder to get a look at Zamora themselves. He is only mildly surprised that the other interested party is also a female. He watches them as they seem to have a heated discussion while gesturing in Zamora's direction. The discussion lasts only a few minutes before the second young lady disappears back the way that she came.

"At least I now have pictures of their faces, and I can try to find out more about them," states Marquise under his breath. He is unaware that Erik is watching his every move very closely, or that he can read lips as well as he can hear.

"I'll have to get those pictures and make some inquiries of my own," states Erik to himself.

Zamora spends another half hour at the market before heading back in the direction of the hotel, however, her return trip is interrupted by a group of orphans begging for handouts. As she tries to understand their rapidly-fired French, Erik walks up to her and tries to shoo the children away unaware that one of the children has a poison dart in his hand that he is supposed to prick Zamora with. However, Marquise notices the child that seems a little out of place when compared to the other beggars he's with, and he makes it a point to get closer to the child without anyone noticing his movements. Just as Erik gets the other children to move out of Zamora's path the little boy makes his move, however, Erik moves in front of Zamora at that moment. Fortunately Marquise was patiently waiting for the child to make his move, and grabs his hand just before the dart strikes Erik in the thigh.

"What the hell," both Zamora and Erik nearly yell at the same time when they see the lightening move made by Marquise.

Marquise, holding the little boy by the wrist, holds up his hand to expose the dart that is hidden between his fingers. Just as Zamora and Erik get a good look at the dart, a local police officer walks up to them with his hand on his firearm. "What is going on here," he asks in heavily accented English. Marquise simply turns the boy's hand so that the officer can see what he's holding. Recognizing the dart for what it is, the officer takes a step back, "Who is the child? And what is the meaning of the dart," he asks sounding somewhat afraid.

"We don't know who he is, or what he intended to do with the dart," states Zamora in perfect French. "The man holding the little boy is part of my security team, and he grabbed the little boy just before the dart pricked my associate Erik who just happened to step in front of me after shooing away some other children," she continues. "What exactly is the dart that he is holding," she asks before becoming silent.

"The dart is more than likely coated in a poison that will kill the person who happens to get pricked by the dart," states the officer speaking in French as well since he is more comfortable speaking in his native

94

language. "So who was the intended victim, you or your associate," the officer asks.

"I believe that the Femme was the intended target," states Marquise. "Erik happened to move in front of her at the last minute as he tried to get one of the children to let go of her clothing," he adds. "I happened to notice that this child didn't look as ragged as the other children, so I decided to see what he was up to," he continues. "And apparently it was a good thing that I did since he is hiding poison darts between his fingers. What shall we do with it," Marquise asks the officer.

"Don't look at me, I'm not touching that thing," states the officer.

Erik then pulls a small plastic bag out of his pocket, dumps the contents into his pocket, and holds the bag up to the little boy's hand. The little boy looks at him defiantly to which Erik states in French, "Drop it." The tone of his voice lets the little boy know that he was not going to be spoken to again, so he reluctantly drops the dart into the bag. "I believe you should be the one to take care of this little device," he states to the officer as he holds out the sealed bag.

The officer reluctantly takes the bag only to have Marquise give him the boy's arm while saying, "I believe this should be placed in your care as well."

While taking hold of the little boy's arm, the officer tells the three of them that he will need them to come to police headquarters and make a statement about the events that have taken place. They agree to meet the officer there after Zamora takes her purchases back to their hotel, and they grab their car. Seemingly somewhat satisfied with their response, the officer leads the boy child to his vehicle parked a short distance away.

When they arrive at the station, the little boy is nowhere to be seen and that makes the trio very nervous. The officer who took the little boy away approaches them with a frown on his face as he asks, "Just who are you people?"

"We are Americans here to do business with your government and IFAN," states Zamora with more than a little annoyance in her voice.

"Why would someone in my country want to kill you," asks the officer.

"That's what we were hoping you would find out," states a very angry Marquise.

"You might want to watch your tone while talking to me," states the officer, getting angry himself.

"I think both of our governments would be interested in today's events," states Zamora as her annoyance increases. "Where is the boy child," she asks.

"I sent him on his way," responds the officer. However, before any of them can respond, he adds, "The boy is an orphan who was paid to prick you with that dart. He does not know the identity of the woman who hired him."

"This is unbelievable," Zamora nearly yells.

"What's the child's name and where can we find him," asks Marquise.

"You are not authorized to interrogate anyone in this country," advises the officer, "And I suggest you do not try to overstep your bounds while you are in My country," he adds. "Now if you all will excuse me this conversation is over," he states as he turns and walks away.

The trio stands there somewhat dumbfounded by the way the officer just dismissed them. Marquise, already devising a plan in his head, takes Zamora's arm and leads her from the police station. What neither of them know, is that Erik is also devising a plan in his head as well. Zamora remains quiet on the ride back to the hotel, and once there goes straight to her room. Marquise and Erik are glad that she wants to be alone so that they can look at the footage from the cameras located in Zamora's clothing. They capture stills of the young lady from the museum, as well as, the young lady she had the heated discussion with at the market place. To their surprise and satisfaction, there is also a good shot of the little boy and the officer on the video. Erik tells Marquise that he will take on the job of sending the photos to Rock so that he can go check on Zamora. Marquise thanks him and heads towards Zamora's room.

Erik goes to his room and lets out a sigh of relief since he was unsure how he was going to get copies of the photos to send to a friend of his that has some very powerful connections. He first takes care of getting the photos to Rock, then he locates the secret compartment in his luggage to retrieve the device he didn't think he would ever have to use. He assembles the device and sends out the necessary message. In no time at all he receives a call.

"Snake Chaser."

"Excalibur."

"Troubles?"

"Info."

"Post."

"Dakar."

"Players?"

"Sending photos."

"Double Time?"

"Precisely."

"Two Clicks."

The line goes dead, and Erik puts away his gear before lying on the bed to contemplate what he has gotten himself into with this assignment. He hopes Snake Chaser can give him some inside information for he sorely needs it. He never thought he would have to take her up on the offer that she made to him ten years ago when he was a thug on the streets of DC.

Heart Body and Soul

Eye Opener

Marquise softly knocks on Zamora's door, however, he doesn't get a response so he just walks in. He finds her sitting in a chair in front of the window just staring into space. She doesn't acknowledge his presence even though he knows that she knows he's entered her room. He walks over and kneels down beside her, and she still doesn't stop staring out the window.

"I know that there have been a lot of things happening that you didn't expect, but you can't lose focus on why we are here," he begins in a soft and soothing voice. When she still doesn't respond, he continues, "I think we really need to take a detailed look at your parent's life to see exactly what their connection is to the missing royal family. Your life may depend on it." She nods slightly acknowledging his words. "I know this is hard on you, but sweetheart I'll be with you every step of the way. I promise I won't let anything happen to you."

Zamora turns to face him, her voice barely above a whisper, "I'm not sure that that is a promise you'll be able to keep," she states. "Someone here wants those artifacts enough to kill people to get them," she adds. "They've already killed my parents, and it looks like they will go to any lengths to kill me." She pauses and takes a deep breath, "I never thought that I would be the focus of an assassination plot when I came over here, and now I'm wondering if I should not have come. But I feel like I owe it to my parents to find out why they died when they came to this country."

Tears are slowly cascading down her face as she speaks her last words, and Marquise's heart goes out to her. He gathers her into his arms, and holds her as she silently cries herself to sleep. He places her on the bed, and lies down beside her not wanting her to wake up alone.

As Marquise lies with Zamora, Erik is waiting for his return call from his contact. When the phone buzzes indicating that a call is coming in, he immediately picks it up and hits the answer button.

"Excalibur."

"Snake Chaser."

"Info."

"How did you get involved with this case?"

"My art background, why?"

"Assassination plots in that country are not easy to stop, damn near impossible. And it seems that the female agent on your case has angered some very influential people by pretending that she is not Princess Zahara."

"If she is Princess Zahara, she's not pretending. She really doesn't know who she is. Apparently her parents never got around to telling her her real history before they were killed. Maybe they thought that their trip here two years ago would be successful and they would tell her when they regained control of their country."

"I tried to tell Zarif and Zarina that it wasn't a good idea for them to go to Africa themselves. They should have sent someone else to negotiate the return of the artifacts. They should have at least let me return with them."

"What? You knew the King and Queen?"

"No, Zarif and Zarina were servants to the King and Queen, and where charged with getting the princess safely out of the country. I was assigned to them when the Princess was recognized by one of her countrymen who was an exchange student at her high school. I was with her until her second year in college when all interest in her ceased. The King and Queen were really killed in the plane crash, but Zahara wasn't with them. The child that died in the crash was the child of a servant."

"So Zamora is really Zahara?"

"Yes she is, and I think you're going to need some invisible help with this case. I can be there in three days. Let you know when I've arrived and I will fill you in on all the details when I get there."

The line goes dead, and Erik sits in stunned silence. He is unsure of what to do with the information that he has just been given or who he should share it with. He then decides he doesn't want anyone to know about his connection to rouge agent Sylvia Williams, so he better keep the information to himself. He will just have to make sure that any plans they make during the course of the case involve strict security for Zamora.

*****

A couple hours later, Zamora awakens from her nap to find herself wrapped in Marquise's arms. When she looks up at his face, he is staring at her with concern written all over his face and something else she can't quite put her finger on. She offers him a weak smile, and he in turn pulls her closer to his body and rests his chin on the top of her head. Neither of them speaks for a long moment.

"I know that you are concerned about your safety, but I will not let anything happen to you," states Marquise still feeling the effects of her earlier statement about not being able to keep his promise to her.

"I know that you will do all that you can to keep me out of harm's way, but I feel like this case is a lot bigger than I originally thought," is her response. "I initiated this case because I wanted to find out what happened to my parents, and I used the black market art dealing as a ruse to get the bureau to open a case here," she continues. "I'm beginning to feel like I'm in over my head, and that this case is turning a little too personal," she adds. "I didn't start this case or come to this country to die, nor did I think that I would be investigating my parent's lives, but now I feel like I don't have a choice. I feel in my gut that there are some things that my parents didn't share with me, and while I know I will have to find out what those things are the thought of it is really starting to scare me." She remains quiet for quite some time, and Marquise keeps silent knowing that she is having some deep thoughts. "What if my parents were the missing King and Queen? What if I am the missing Princess? What is going to become of the life that I have known for the past twenty-eight years?"

"We will deal with the answers to your questions as they are revealed," replies Marquise knowing that she was just voicing her concerns out loud. "No decisions have to be made at this moment," he adds. He hears her long sigh, and continues to hold her in his arms for a few more moments. "Alright, we have lain in this bed long enough. It is time for us to get up and start planning our strategy," he states, "and for me to let you in on a little secret." He looks her in the face to see what her reaction is to his last statement. He notes the arching of her eyebrow and the spark of anger in her eyes before continuing. "I planted some micro cameras into some of your garments so that we could watch whoever is watching you," he begins. He feels her anger escalate, and tightens his hold on her. "We were able to get good shots of the boy child and the officer that Erik should have already sent to Rock, so we should know their identity soon," he adds while making a conscious decision not to tell her about the young lady from the museum or her friend.

"I'm glad to hear that the cameras have provided us with a means of gaining information about the people out to kill me, but I'm not happy to hear that they were planted on me without my knowledge," is her response.

102

"We didn't want to you to become overly concerned about your own safety, but we wanted to be able to identify all the players in this game of cat and mouse," he states. "Plus we felt if you knew the cameras were there, you would try to capture too much and that your movements might give away the fact that you were doing surveillance work while out and about which might have caused the assassins to back off," he adds.

"You have a point so I'll check my anger and annoyance this time, but in the future I would like to be kept informed of all actions taking place."

"You got it sweetheart," he responds. "Besides at this point I think it's best that you do know everything, just in case neither Erik nor I are close enough to stop another attempt on your life." He feels the shudder that runs through her body, and gives her a squeeze. "I don't want to scare you, but I think you need to well informed about everything that has to do with this case."

"I know. It's just that the thought that someone wants me dead is a little unsettling, especially since I don't know why they want me dead." She angles her head and places a kiss on his chin before trying to un-entangle her body from his, "You're right, we've lain here long enough. Let's get back in the game."

Change in Strategy

All three agents enter the living area at the same time just as all of their phones start chirping. It's a message from Rock telling them to come to the compound ASAP. Knowing it has something to do with the pictures and the attempt on Zamora's life, they waste no time getting dressed and head right over.

Once they arrive, Rock ushers them into a small sound proof room. "I'm sure you know why I summoned you here, so I'm just going to get down to it," begins Rock.

"The male child that tried to prick you with dart is from the village of Gamboto, and more than likely was sent by the royal family there to get rid of you," states Rock directly to Zamora. "The officer at the scene also has direct ties to the Gamboto tribe, and that is probably the reason he sent the child on his way before you arrived," he continues, talking to all three of them. He takes a deep breath before turning to look at Zamora directly, "I think there is something that you should know, and you're not going to like." As she turns to look at Marquise and Erik, he adds, "If my hunches about these two are right, they already know and weren't sure if the information should be shared with you. However, I think it's in the best interest of this case if you know." He takes another deep breath as he moves to stand directly in front of her, "You are the missing Princess Zahara."

Zamora is stunned. She doesn't breathe, she doesn't blink. She just stands there staring at Rock. "Baby girl I hate to spring it on you like this, but it's the truth." She still doesn't respond.

Marquise, feeling overly protective, nudges Rock out of the way and takes both of her hands in his. He notes how cold her hands feel, and that she still doesn't appear to be breathing. He pulls her close to him, which sends her into overdrive. She pushes him away from her, and looks at all three of them assessing if the other two indeed did already know. She can tell by their concerned looks that they did indeed know. The anger in her eyes is evident. "How long," she asks in an angry whisper.

Rock is the first to speak, "Last night."

Zamora then turns to Erik. "I found out today."

Lastly she turns to Marquise, "I made some inquires the day we arrived at the hotel." As her eyes narrow on him, he holds up both of his hands, "None of what I found out was truly confirmed until just now though," he continues. "That's why I asked you to consider the possibility that you were the princess so if it was confirmed you wouldn't be shocked," he adds.

Satisfied that she wasn't purposely kept in the dark by her team and mentor, she sinks down into a chair as the impact of the information she just received sinks in. "How? Why didn't they tell me?"

Rock is the first to speak, "First Yafar and Yamina were not your parents." Zamora's head snaps up, but she doesn't speak. "Yafar and Yamina were your parent's personal servants. The King and Queen gave you over to their care and took a village child with them when they were leaving the country," he continues. "They were worried that an attempt would be made on your lives, and they didn't want you to be with them in case the attempt was successful," he adds. "As I am sure you've figured out, yes your parents were killed in that plan crash, but you survived and were brought to the US by Zarif and Zarina which are Yafar and Yamina's real names. They were given specific instructions on how you were to be brought up in case your parents did not make it safely out of Africa. They were also given specific instructions on when to come back to this country to allow you to regain control of your country. However, they were killed before they could complete their task. No one anticipated that the countrymen here would mistake them as the King and Queen, although they did somewhat favor your parents as they were distant relatives."

Rock pauses in order to give Zamora time to process the information that he has shared with her at this point. Marquise kneels down in front of her and takes her hands in his again, still noting how cold they feel. He begins rubbing first one hand and then the other trying to get her blood circulating again. She looks up at him with a vacant look in her eyes, "Oh hell," he states before picking her up, taking her seat, and placing her on his lap while wrapping his arms around her. Knowing that she needs time, Rock and Erik leave the room.

Marquise sits there for over thirty minutes giving Zamora time to process what she's heard before he speaks. "Sweetheart," he whispers. She lifts her head off his shoulder to look into his eyes. He sees a trace of disbelief in her eyes, "I know that this is hard to fathom, but all the evidence indicates that you are indeed the missing princess. I'm sure that someone can fill you in on all the missing details, but in the meantime we are going to have to change our strategy to keep you out of harm's way. You understand that, right?"

She nods her head, not willing to trust her voice at this point. She lays her head back on his chest for a few minutes before taking a deep breath, at which point she stands up. The vacant look that was previously in her eyes is replaced with determination, and Marquise braces himself for the hurricane that he is sure she is going to unleash on him and the others. However, before she can say a word in walks Rock and Erik. "You boys are right on time," she states as they close the door behind them.

"Czar," begins Rock. "Before you go on the tirade I'm sure you're gearing up for, let me have my say first."

"Contrary to what you all believe, there is no tirade forth coming. However, I do want to know what the new plan is, as I'm sure there is one." At their collective looks of disbelief, she states, "Oh, I have no desire to die before this case is solved, so you all can rest assure that I will follow whatever plan you've come up with to the letter. However, I make no such assurances once this case is solved."

The three men look at one another in apprehension of what they will face once the case is solved. However, they know they have a job to do for the time being, and they need to bring Zamora up to speed. "GL will now become a permanent member of your team," begins Rock. At Zamora's arched brow, he holds up a hand to silence her as he continues, "His presence can be explained as the US Government wanting to make sure no more attempts are made against your life as you are a US Citizen. We are hoping that his presence in your entourage will cause the Gambotos to think twice about making another attempt against you." Rock then moves to the projector and turns it on. As the images appear on the screen, Rock informs them that they are looking at the members of the Gamboto tribe, as well as, their known hench men.

"They're just children," gasps Zamora when the images of five children appear on the screen.

"And they are the most deadly as most people who see them see them as children, and not a threat to their safety," responds Rock. "So be especially careful about any children who approach any of you," states Rock to all three of them. At that moment GL enters the room, "Right on time GL," states Rock. "I was just informing the team about who they should be watchful of while walking the streets of the village."

"Great," states GL. "I will be staying in the hotel across the street from yours," he states to the team. "However, I will be traveling with you whenever you venture out into the village. We're hoping seeing a US dignitary with you when you are out and about will make people think twice about you being the princess, and about making attempts on your life. We are confident that the citizens of this country do not want to make war with ours, and after the death of your parents they know another US citizen dying on their soil will bring an army down upon them."

The team sits down and goes over their strategy for the remainder of their stay in Dakar. Once they are sure everyone knows their roles, they head back to the hotel.

*****

Once in their suite, Erik states that he has a headache and is going to lay down for a bit. As soon as he closes the door to his room, he pulls out his other cell to see if he has received word from the agent known as Snake Chaser. He has received word. She is in the country and wants to meet with him on the outskirts of the village in one hour. He gets his gear together for the meeting. When he emerges from his room, he is surprised to see Zamora and Marquise sitting in the living area drinking coffee.

"Where are you going," asks Marquise as he takes note of Erik's gear pack.

"It's too stuffy in here," begins Erik. "I'm hoping some fresh air will do me good. Since we know what we're up against here, I thought it best I be prepared in case someone decides that there are too many people surrounding Zamora, and decides to get rid of me," he adds as he sees both Zamora and Marquise eyeing is gear pack.

Zamora simply nods, but he can see the questions in Marquise's eyes. "I'll be fine," he tries to reassure Marquise.

"Fine. Call us if you run into anything while you're out there," states Marquise.

"Will do," responds Erik before heading out of the suite.

Heart Body and Soul

Subterfuge

While lying in each other's arms, the King and Queen are thinking about what the American said during his visit. The King speaks first, "What if Orogotto's plans to get the artifacts don't go as planned," he asks as he leans up to look in his wife's face. "We should have an alternate plan, and maybe we can use the American if he proves reliable."

"I too am concerned that Orogotto might not be successful, but I am not sure about the American," responds the Queen. "I do not like the feeling I got when we met with him. There is something very unsettling about him," she adds.

"I agree with you on that," responds the King. "However, I think we can still use him to get the artifacts, and then we can dispose of him. If he is a traitor to his country, I don't think that they will make a big deal out of his death or disappearance."

"You are probably right dear husband. What should be our first move?"

"I will get word to Orogotto to set up a meet with the American at the museum as I don't think anyone would think twice about either of us visiting the museum at the same time." After a brief pause, he continues, "After I am sure that the American can deliver the artifacts and the necessary paperwork, Orogotto and I will devise a plan to get rid of the American. And I will devise a plan to make sure Orogotto shoulders the blame if anything goes awry. I do not want any of this to reflect badly on our kingdom, nor do I want it to stop us from gaining control of Umboto."

"I will leave all the planning up to you," states the Queen. "Just let me know if you need me to participate in any way."

The King kisses her on the forehead as way of saying thanks for always standing behind him 100%. "I will let you know if you are needed." With that, he gets up and gets dressed so that he can begin to put his plans in motion.

*****

The King enters his office and calls upon his most trusted agents. Once they arrive and are seated around his desk, he fills them in.

"As you know the Royal Umboto Artifacts are on their way to this country, and I need to get my hands on them," he begins. "The museum curator, Orogotto, has assured me that he can get his hands on the artifacts and can stake a claim as the rightful owner. He is also willing to marry Princess Shimira to join our two nations," he continues. "However, I am not as confident in his abilities as he is," he adds. "The Queen and I were paid a visit today by an American who claims that he too can get his hands on the artifacts, and legitimately turn them over to us which will give us rule over the Umboto Kingdom," he further adds. "However, I am not sure of his abilities or trustworthiness either. So we will devise a plan to thwart any underhanded dealings by either of them. If things do not go as planned, I want the American take care of, and all of the blame to be placed on the shoulders of Orogotto."

The men nod their heads in understanding, and King Gamboto lays out the details of his plans, as well as, the role that each of them is to play. He informs them this may be their last chance to join the two kingdoms together, so everything must go as planned.

Heart Body and Soul

Reunions

Zamora and Marquise continue to quietly sip their coffee as they watch Erik close the door behind him, until the atmosphere around them seems to grow warmer by the second. They both feel the sexual energy surrounding them at the same time, and turn to look into each other's eyes. What Marquise sees in Zamora's eyes stops his breathing, and he notices how still her chest becomes as he is sure the same thing is reflected in his eyes as well. An all consuming desire that neither one of them has the power to stop takes over the room. Marquise's tongue and fingers start tingling in anticipation of tasting and touching her all over, and his thoughts are visible in his eyes. Zamora is unable to control the shiver that races through her body as she sees all of what Marquise intends to do to her all over his face. They both set their coffee cups on the table at the same time, and then Marquise swoops her up in his arms and carries her to her bedroom sets her on her feet. He undresses her, staring into her eyes the whole time, before he lays her in the middle of the bed. He continues to stare into her eyes as he undresses, and she is powerless to do anything but watch.

"Enjoying the show," he asks in a voice filled with desire. All Zamora can do is lick her lips in anticipation of tasting him all over. "I'll take that as a yes," he states as his desire rises to a level it's never been before. Once he is standing before her in all his natural glory, Zamora gets on her knees and crawls to the edge of the bed. She reaches out and circles her nail around his nipple, and upon hearing his sharp intake of breath she replaces

111

her nail with her tongue. Marquise's hands are balled into tight fists at his side as he lets her enjoy her time tormenting and torturing his body. Zamora trails her tongue down the center of his chest, across his abdomen, and down to his hip. She feels the trembles cascading through his body as he barely holds on to his sanity while she savors the taste of his skin. As the tip of her tongue circles the head of his throbbing, hard organ, he lets out a groan from deep in his chest while clinching his fists tighter. At the sound of his groan, she takes him completely into her mouth and he loses it. He grabs her under her arms and gently pushes her back on the bed as he enters her in one complete thrust.

"Marquise!"

"Zamora!"

Once the thrill of the initial entry settles around them, he strokes her for all he's worth bringing them both to completion in no time at all. The first orgasm is so powerful that he hardens again instantly, and proceeds to thoroughly make love to her. Zamora instantly falls asleep at the end of their love making, and Marquise just lays there staring at her wondering how he is going to survive leaving her behind. He knows that it's inevitable as she is an African Princess, and he will not fit into her life here in her native country. Not knowing how long he'll be able to enjoy holding her in his arms while she sleeps, he lays down beside her and gathers her close to his side before succumbing to the call for sleep himself.

*****

Erik reaches the rendezvous point, however, he doesn't see his contact person. He double checks his phone to make sure that he is in the right spot, and just as he raises his head he sees the sand in front of him shifting. He is momentarily stunned as he sees a figure emerging from the shifting sand, however, he quickly recovers as he notices that the person is his contact.

"Snake Chaser," he states when she moves to stand in front of him.

"Excalibur," is her response. They hug each other in greeting before they get down to business. "I thought I taught you never to show emotion when on a case," she admonishes with very little heat in her voice.

"Sylvia, you never cease to amaze me with your abilities to camouflage yourself in your surroundings," states Erik.

"And you are still a Green Horn," she responds with laughter in her voice. "I have secured us a private location where we can talk," she states as she turns and walks towards what appears to be a mound of sand.

When they reach the mound of sand, he sees the opening from which Sylvia emerged. They both enter the hole, and she proceeds to lead him to her underground hideout. Anxious to know the full story and Sylvia's plan of action, Erik wastes no time in speaking, "First tell me your plan of action, then you can tell me the story from the beginning."

Sylvia chuckles before asking, "What makes you think I have a plan of action?"

Erik cocks an eyebrow before responding, "Cause I know you. And I'm sure that you already know all the players on the continent, and what their roles are. So again, what's your plan of action?"

Sylvia chuckles again before asking, "You think you know me quite well don't you?" At the nod of his head and his smile, she continues, "In this case you do. I do have a plan of action, but it's going to require some highly qualified individuals to pull it off. Who is here on this case with you?"

"Heading up the case is Rick Price," he responds.

"Rock is good. Glad he's here."

"Then there's Giovanni . . .".

"Swamp Rat," shrieks Sylvia before Erik could finish saying the name. "Definitely glad that he's here." Sylvia chuckles at the scowl that Erik is giving her for interrupting him. "You may continue without further interruption," she states.

"Thank you," he states sarcastically. "There's Enrique Whittmore, a new guy Marquise McMillan, and of course the princess who is known to the agency as Zamora Richardson and as Zariah Robinson on this mission."

"Pathfinder is with the agency now," asks a slightly stunned Sylvia. She quickly recovers, however, as she ponders the other name Erik gave her. "Not excited that Sidewinder is here though."

"Who don't you know," asks a slightly surprised Erik.

"There are a few people out there that I don't know, but good people I tend to make sure I know and know well, as well as people that I need to keep both eyes on and Sidewinder is one of those you should keep three eyes on," she responds. "But if I know Pathfinder as well as I think that I do, he has just the crew that we need close by," she continues. She begins pacing as she reviews her plan in her head and how to get Pathfinder on board without him being pissed about being asked to go off the grid with being new to the agency. "Do you think you could get Pathfinder to come meet with us without telling him who he's meeting with?" At Erik's cocked eyebrow, she continues, "He's somewhat of a straight arrow, and I'm not sure if he would be willing to go off the grid if this is his first major case with the agency."

Understanding where she's coming from, "I don't think that you will have any problem getting him to go off grid on this case," he states. At Sylvia's cocked eyebrow, he elaborates, "He's in love with the princess." At Sylvia's stunned silence, he adds, "I don't know the whole story of how they met, but they know each other quite well. I think that she is as much in love with him as he is with her."

114

"I'm not sure if that's a good thing or a bad thing," muses Sylvia out loud. "Pathfinder in love, never thought I would see the day that would happen," she continues musing. However, she regroups quickly, "We might be able to make that work in our favor," she states. "Now here's the plan," she states as she sits down and begins pulling documents out of her duffle bag.

They sit down for an hour going over everything that Sylvia has brought with her. Just before leaving, Erik states, "I think Marquise will be on board without a problem, and will be able to handle it without love clouding his thoughts." At her nod, he continues, "I'll bring them back in an hour." He then leaves the way that he came.

Reunions II

Unable to quiet his mind, Marquise wakes up a short time later, and Erik returns to the hotel just as Marquise is emerging from Zamora's room. "Hey man," states Erik, "I need to talk to you." At Marquise's nod, he continues, "I just met with a friend of yours, and she's here to help."

"A friend of mine," asks Marquise skeptically.

"Snake Chaser," is Erik's simple response.

Marquise lifts an eyebrow in surprise, "That's a name I haven't heard in years," he responds. "How do you know her, and why is she here?"

"We met years ago when I was a kid on the streets of DC getting into trouble. She changed my life," he answers. "I sent for her. And before you go Rambo on me, I would trust her with my life and I thought that we might need her expertise on this mission. I've seen her in action."

"Not going Rambo," responds Marquise on a chuckle. "I'm actually glad she's here. We're going to need all the help we can get, and she's one of the best. Have you set up a meet?"

"Yes," is Erik's automatic response. "This was a lot easier than I thought that it would be. I think Zamora should come to the meet as well."

"I agree. She needs to be a part of everything from now on. Her life depends on it."

"You're deeply in love with her aren't you?"

"Unfortunately, I am."

"Why unfortunately?"

"Because when this mission is over, she will have to remain here to run her country, and I will be returning to the states."

"Why can't you stay here with her? I know she's in love with you too."

"That's not how things work here. This country and its royalty operate a whole lot differently than we do in the states. She has a responsibility to her people to make the right alliances to ensure their prosperity and protection, and I won't interfere with that." Marquise closes his eyes and takes a deep breath as the reality of the situation settles around him. He doesn't notice the slight crack in Zamora's door closing, however, Erik does. He smiles on the inside because he has a feeling that Zamora will not willingly go along with Marquise's plans for after the mission.

"If he thinks I'm letting him get away from me after this mission is over, I have news for him," she mumbles under her breath as she makes her way to the bathroom to get cleaned up.

Erik retreats to his room to put his gear away and prepare for the meet with Sylvia, Marquise, and Zamora. Marquise enters his room to do the same thing.

Erik, Marquise, and Zamora enter the common area of their suite at the same time. "Ready," they all state at once. Marquise and Erik are slightly confused about what Zamora thinks they should be ready for, so they ask her.

"The meet with Snake Chaser of course," is her response.

"How do you know about that," asks Marquise.

"She was listening at the door when we were talking earlier," answers Erik before Zamora could say a word. As Marquise spins on Zamora, Erik states, "I'll give you two a few minutes," before going back inside his room.

Before Marquise can say one word, Zamora firmly states, "We will discuss us when the mission is over." When Marquise doesn't respond, she continues, "Right now I want to concentrate on saving my life and finding the people who killed my parents. All four of them."

Marquise understands what she is saying and knows it's true, so he merely nods before calling out to Erik. Erik exits his room, and they all head to the meet with Sylvia.

Erik takes them to the beach where he and Sylvia met earlier that night, and simply grins at the blank look on Zamora face. Neither he nor Marquise so much as twitch when the sand starts to shift, but Zamora has to use her hand to cover the small gasp that came across her lips. When Sylvia emerges, Zamora feels a twinge of recognition but has no time to dwell on it as everyone starts moving in Sylvia's direction. Once inside her hideout, Sylvia introduces herself to Zamora while wondering how long it's going to take her to remember when and where they have met.

Sylvia and Marquise share a hug of friendship and remembrance. "Long time Pathfinder."

"Yes. It has been Snake Chaser. When are you going to stop being a chameleon and start to heal?"

"I won't be able to heal until he is caught. You know that," she responds before turning to her make shift table and the papers laid out on top of it.

Sylvia clears her throat of the emotion she is feeling at the memory of losing her fiancé. "I assume Cockroach is aware and nearby," states Sylvia while turning in Marquise's direction.

"You assume correctly," responds Marquise.

"Great! His team will become critical in order for us to pull this off, and for me to remain off the grid." She then tilts her head in what Marquise knows to be her *I-will-not-be-swayed* position. What Sylvia and the rest weren't prepared for was that it would spark recognition in Zamora.

Before she could catch herself, Zamora yells out, "YOU!" She quickly clamps her lips shut when everyone turns in her direction at her outburst.

Before anyone can say a word, Sylvia moves directly in front of Zamora before stating, "Yes Czar, it's me. I was wondering how long it would take you to recognize me." On a chuckle she states, "Should have known the look would have done it since I perfected it while watching out for your safety." The chuckle is quickly cut off as Zamora grabs her in a big bear hug, and nearly squeezes the life out of her. "Czar," she barely gets out, "I can't breathe."

Zamora quickly let's her go, "Sorry. I'm just so happy to see you. I was actually praying for you when I found out that I was the missing princess, and here you are."

"I told you that I would never be far, and would always be there for you if you ever needed me," states Sylvia.

"Yes, yes you did." Quickly recovering from her shock and relief, Zamora states, "What's the set up?"

"Hold on," states Marquise at after recovering from the shock that Sylvia and Zamora know each other. "Care to explain that little exchange," demands Marquise with a scowl on his face.

Sylvia and Zamora look at each other and chuckle, then Zamora nods to Sylvia who explains how they know each other. "I was assigned to Zamora while she was in high school, and one of her country men recognized her on campus. We needed to protect her identity, and discourage any unwanted interest in her." At Marquise's raised eyebrow, she adds, "As I'm sure you discovered, Czar is a handful, and she was probably even more so back then hating all the restrictions that were placed upon her with no explanation. She knew her parents were wealthy, but she didn't think that it warranted all the extra security that was around."

"We can get to everyone's story after the mission is over," interrupts Zamora, "Let's get to the plan so we can end this thing, and I don't have to sleep with one eye open."

"See what I mean," states Sylvia on a chuckle. At Zamora's glare, she holds up her hands, "Okay, I give. Let's get to it."

Sylvia looks at Marquise and Erik to fill her in from their end. Marquise takes the lead and speaks first, "These are the people we believe we have to watch out for when on the streets," he states as he pulls up the pictures on the handheld device he received from Rock.

"I see they're still using children to do their dirty work," states Sylvia as she goes through the photos. "Tell me what events have taken place since your arrival," she then asks.

Marquise and Erik inform her of all the events that have taken place, and the measures that they have taken to keep Zamora safe. Marquise also informs everyone about the Navy men he has positioned nearby lead by one of his most trusted soldiers, codename Cockroach for his ability to survive just about anything and penetrate any structure undetected. "Rock cannot know of Cockroach's presence or yours for that matter," states Marquise directly to Sylvia.

"I'm well aware that he cannot know that I am here," states Sylvia somewhat annoyed. "I am here because Excalibur sent for me, and
120

because Zamora needs me. And believe me I plan to make sure that she remains safe, as well as, maintaining my invisibility with the agency until I find Qasean's killer and do what the agency refuses to do," she ends on a near growl.

"Settle down Sylvia," begins Marquise, "I just want to make sure we are all in agreement as to who needs to know what in this case. Things are going to get decidedly more complicated before this thing is over, and I plan to make sure that we all make it out of here alive and in one piece. Okay?"

"Fine," responds Sylvia, "Let's get back to the plan."

The Set Up

"The artifacts are due to arrive in this country in 11 days, right," asks Sylvia.

"That is correct," answers Zamora.

"We know that there are five possible assassins, and the fact that they are all children will make it difficult to apprehend them without arousing suspicions. However, I think I can work an angle I've used in this country before," begins Sylvia. "I've posed as a photographer documenting African Culture in the past, so I think I can resurrect that role as my reason for being in the country right now," she continues. "You probably won't recognize me on the street if you see me, but I will make it a point to be in the village anytime that you are out and about," she adds. "I think it's best that Swamp Rat and Sidewinder not know that I am here, and on the case," she concludes.

"What about Cockroach," asks Marquise.

"Yes, let him know as he will be critical to the plan, and we need to coordinate our efforts so that he can take credit for the takedown if it comes down to that," she responds.

"What is your plan," asks Zamora.

"I don't think that they will make anymore attempts on your life until the artifacts arrive since they believe that the US Government is closely watching them after Sidewinder and Swamp Rat's visits to the Museum Curator," responds Sylvia. "However, I will arrive in the country in two days time with my journalism credentials in place. I will get a room in the same hotel as Swamp Rat so that I can have a clear view of your hotel," she adds. "Upon my arrival, I will begin photographing children from various villages, but will eventually take a keen interest in these five children from the Gamboto tribe. If I'm successful in convincing the tribe that I can gain interest in their country by capturing the lives of these children, I will be able to make sure that they are out of the area the day the artifacts arrive. However, that may lead the Gamboto leaders to look to older assassins to go after Zamora, so you will have to be watchful of every member of the tribe at that point."

Zamora, Marquise, and Erik all nod in understanding, as Sylvia continues, "That's where Cockroach comes into play," she states in Marquise's direction. His team will need to position themselves throughout the city from the docks to the museum, and at your hotel. They should divide up into teams of three with at least one sharp shooter on each team, as well as, someone who can blend into the surroundings undetected."

"I don't think that will be a problem," responds Marquise. "I'll let him know of the plan when we return to the hotel."

"In the meantime, stick with your original plans while waiting for the artifacts to arrive," adds Sylvia. "Don't want the natives to think that we're on to them or that we're even here."

"No problem," responds Marquise before turning to Zamora and Erik, "I think it's time that we head back to the hotel."

They nod in agreement, and take their leave of Sylvia.

*****

Once back at the hotel, Marquise heads to his room to make contact with Cockroach leaving Erik and Zamora alone in the living room.

"Tell me if I'm out of line, but you love him deeply don't you," asks Erik.

"You are out of line," responds Zamora without the heat Erik was expecting. "But you are right, I do love him deeply. However, I don't think that will alter his decision to return to the states without me once this is all over," she adds. After a moment of silence, she continues, "Not sure what to do about that."

"It's obvious that the two of you met before stepping foot in Africa and that you were both surprised to see one another here, how is that possible?"

"We met two years ago on a stretch of highway in Georgia, and neither one of us expected to see each other again after that encounter. He was a sheriff then, and didn't know that I was an agent. Nor did I know that he had applied for a position with the agency," she finishes on a broken voice. Suddenly silent tears start running down her face, and she moves to look out the window to the street below.

Sensing that she needed a moment to collect herself, Erik remains seated on the couch quietly waiting for her to speak again. Zamora regains her composure, and resumes her seat on the couch. "I need you to make me a promise, and this has to stay between the two of us," whispers Zamora. Erik simply quirk's his eyebrow in response. "If this mission doesn't end the way that we want, make sure that Marquise doesn't blame himself if anything happens to me. Promise me that?"

"Whoa," responds Erik while jumping up off the couch. "That's a really big promise you're asking for considering how much that man loves you," he begins. "He's already hurting knowing that he will have to leave you behind to govern your country when this mission is over, and I'm hoping that the fact that you're alive and well will help ease his pain over time." He pauses and runs his hand down his face before continuing, "However, if you didn't survive, I don't think that this country would survive for he

124

would tear it apart trying to find the person that caused you harm. And then he would mourn you for the rest of his life. So, how about we make a pact to keep you alive instead? I think that would be easier to achieve."

"I would love nothing more that to still be breathing when this is all over, but I have to be realistic about this. This plot against me could be bigger than we know, and we might not have all the angles covered."

"I think Sylvia and Marquise are going to ensure that all angles are covered, so don't worry about that."

Thinking that she wasn't going to get anywhere with Erik tonight, she turns towards her room, "I think I'll go lay down for a while."

"Sweet dreams," states Erik as she enters her room. He then retreats to his room as well to rest since he figures the next eleven days are going to be rough on everyone.

*****

Inside his room Marquise makes contact with Cockroach.

"Cockroach."

"Pathfinder."

"Time?"

"Deadly Stealth. Three by Three. Eleven days."

"Anything else?"

"Snake Chaser."

"What?"

"History with Princess. Details later."

"You're covered."

The line goes dead, and Marquise runs his hand down his face as he knows that no matter the outcome, he has no future with the woman who holds his heart. He lies across the bed to gather his thoughts and emotions before going to see Zamora. Before he knows it, he's fallen asleep and dreaming of her.

Unable to sleep for thoughts of Marquise, Zamora makes her way to his room only find him sleeping fully dressed. Wanting to be next to him, she starts to undress him and he never awakens as he thinks it's all a dream. However, when he feels her lips and tongue bringing him to life, he suddenly awakens because it feels so real. To his surprise it is real. He tries to disengage himself from her mouth, but she simply grips him tighter in her hand and continues loving him with her mouth. Knowing that he won't be able to get her to stop, he lies back down and grips the sheets on the bed and lets her enjoy her feast. Just as he's ready to climax, he pulls her up over him pulls her panties to the side and impels her with himself. Gripping her hips tightly he pumps every bit of his essence inside of her which causes her to climax as well.

Once she regains the ability to speak, she places a finger across his lips so that he can't interrupt her. "If you think I'm letting you go when this over, you better think again." He tries to speak, but she simply covers his mouth with hers and kisses him till she feels him getting hard again inside of her. They make love throughout the night.

Heart Body and Soul

Snake In The Grass

For the next two days, there seems to be very little activity by the Gambotos even though Zamora has spent quite a bit of time exploring the country side and the various villages. Marquise, Erik, and Giovanni have been keeping their eyes wide open for any unusual people and children in the streets near their hotels. Monsieur Orogotto has been spending all of his time making sure that he has the right cases to display the artifacts when they arrive, and double and triple checking the security that will be in place to guard the artifacts while in his care. Sareena has been keeping close tabs on Orogotto's movements and preparations, as well as, those of Zamora and her travel companions.

Sylvia arrives without so much as a ripple, and immediately begins surveillance on all parties involved beginning with the curator and his staff while she photographs the children that are begging on the steps of the museum. She is somewhat surprised to see Sidewinder entering the museum on the third day of her stakeout, but what shocks her most is that the head of the Gamboto tribe enters the museum less than five minutes later.

"What the hell is going on here," she mutters to herself. Determined to get some answers, she enters the museum. "Greetings," she states to Sareena who rolls her eyes at the thought of another American being at the museum. Choosing to ignore the sarcasm dripping from the young lady, Sylvia asks, "Are pictures allowed to be taken inside the museum?"

"Why would you want to take pictures in here?"

"The architecture of the building is amazing, and I would like to capture it on film."

Not really caring about the American or her camera, Sareena simply waves her on, "Take all the pictures you like."

Sylvia, pleased with being dismissed by the woman, begins exploring the museum snapping pictures until she is completely forgotten about. Relying on her ability to blend into her surroundings and already having a layout of the museum, she makes her way back to the office of the curator since she's sure that's where the men are meeting. Once there she hears a heated conversation taking place between Enrique "Sidewinder" Whittmore and the Head of the Gamboto tribe.

"I thought that you were going to make sure that the American woman was taken care of," she hears Sidewinder say heatedly.

"The first attempt brought a lot of attention our way," replies Gamboto, "We are going to have to bide our time, but she will be taken care of," he adds. "Besides you were supposed to be getting us inside information on her movements. Are you doing your part?"

"Unfortunately, I have been left out of the loop at the moment," Enrique responds. "I have been left out of the last few meetings just in case your people get too close to her, as my government doesn't want your people to know what my true role is here."

"Well, that is unfortunate. You are not proving to be as useful as you claimed you would be when you first approached us," responds Orogotto.

"I will get you the information that you require to dispose of the woman, you just make sure you have my money when this is over," Enrique heatedly responds. He then storms out of the office without noticing the young woman with the camera in the hallway.

Sylvia quietly follows him out of the museum, and notes that he is headed in the opposite direction of his hotel. "Hmm, seems there is another snake in the grass surrounding the Princess. I'll have to make provisions for him," she says to herself. Feeling as though her work at the museum is complete for the day, she heads back to her hotel room as she needs to get this new bit of information to Marquise and Erik.

*****

Meditating in his room, Erik is surprised when he hears the faint chirp of his cell that connects him to Sylvia. He picks it up and enters the code to open up communication.

"Excalibur."

"Snake Chaser."

"Development?"

"New snake in the grass."

"Who?"

"Hideaway. Nightfall. All hands."

The line is disconnected, and Erik simply stares at the phone for a few minutes before putting it away. He then seeks out Marquise and Zamora.

"It seems Sylvia has uncovered another player, and wants to meet with us at nightfall."

"Shit," hisses Marquise. "Who the hell could this be?"

"I guess we'll have to wait for nightfall to find out," states Zamora a lot calmer than she's actually feeling. When both men turn in her direction, she simply shrugs her shoulders, "Until we know who it is, there's not much we can do. So I'm not going to get upset about it in the meantime."

Realizing that she's right, both men blow out a frustrated breath before having a seat. "Who else in this country has something to gain by gaining control of the artifacts besides the Gambotos," asks Marquise out loud.

"No one that I know of," responds Erik, "but I'll see what I can find out from my contacts in the art world." He then heads back to his room.

Marquise pats his lap as an indication that he wants Zamora to have a seat there. Once she perches herself on his lap, he wraps his arms around her before saying, "You are taking this all in stride despite the seriousness of all that is taking place around you."

"I have to keep a level head about this mission, despite my personal connection to it, if we are all going to be alive to talk about it when it's over."

"I suppose you are right, however, I hate the fact that someone wants you dead. I feel like I have a dagger just inches from my heart, and one wrong move will send it deep into my flesh." He frames her face in his hands, "I'm sure you already know, but just in case you don't," he pauses for effect, "I love you with all my heart, and I don't know if I would survive if something happened to you." Before she can say one word, he steals her breath with a kiss she feels all the way to her toes. When he breaks off the kiss, he places a finger over her lips, before saying, "Don't say a word. I just wanted you to know that." When it appears she's going to speak anyway, he replaces his finger with his lips once again. This time when the kiss ends, Zamora decides to let him have his way, this time. She lays her head on his chest, and they stay that way until Erik enters the room.

Having accepted the personal nature of Zamora and Marquise's relationship, Erik is not affected by Zamora being in Marquise's arms. "They only thing I was able to learn is that there has been talk about some missing African Artifacts being up for bid on the Black Market," begins Erik. "And it seems the highest bid was made by Monsieur Orogotto," he continues. "Zamora, are you sure that the artifacts are secure where they are?"

"Of course they're safe," Zamora responds sarcastically.

"I'm only asking because it seems that someone out there believes that they can get their hands on them, and plans to sell them to Orogotto at a high price."

"There is no way that anyone could get their hands on those artifacts before they arrive in this country," states Zamora. "And once they arrive they will be guarded round the clock by members of the NSA, CIA, and FBI. So I don't see how anyone would be able to gain access to them, unless . . .", continues Zamora until she becomes quiet as she is consumed by her own thoughts.

"Unless what," asks Marquise and Erik simultaneously.

"Unless someone from our team plans to steal them and sell them to the museum," she begins. "But they can't possibly believe that they would be able to get away with it."

"We have some highly trained individuals on this case who are experts at hiding just about anything including themselves," responds Marquise.

"Very true," responds Zamora. "I guess we'll have to wait and see what Sylvia has uncovered."

*****

Nightfall arrives, and the three of them make their way to Sylvia's hideout.

"I'm going to come right out with it since time is of the essence here," begins Sylvia. "Sidewinder has plans to steal the artifacts and sell them to the museum curator."

"What," yell Marquise, Erik, and Zamora at the same time.

"Are you sure," asks Zamora who is having a hard time maintaining her temper.

"Yes, I overheard him, the head of the Gamboto tribe, and the monsieur discussing it at the museum earlier today."

"Shit," Marquise mutters heatedly.

"So what can we do to stop him," asks Erik trying to remain calm with this latest bit of news.

"I can take him out of the equation, and force the hand of the Gambotos," responds Sylvia. As the other three turn in her direction with raised eyebrows, she continues, "The artifacts are due to arrive at the museum in six days, so we don't have a lot of time to figure out how he plans to get his hands on them. However, if we get rid of him, then Gamboto and the curator will have to find another way to get their hands on them." She pauses for a few minutes knowing that her next words are not going to be received well, "However, once he is out of the picture, I'm sure that the efforts to assassinate Zamora will more than double."

Knowing that the words just spoken are extremely accurate, the room becomes deathly quiet. Everyone is lost in their own thoughts of how this could play out, and no one is pleased by the most prevalent thought – these people want Zamora dead so that they can claim the rights to her country.

Decisions

After having explored their own personal thoughts for some time, Marquise speaks first. "How do we dispose of Enrique without informing Rock?"

"That does pose a problem," states Sylvia, "for he cannot know of my involvement."

"I think we should leave Enrique in play so as to flush out everyone involved in the deal he's made, and then we don't have to tell Rock anything," states Erik. "Our main focus here should be to keep Zamora alive which means we need to know everyone who would stand to gain something from her death. We also don't need to spook any of the players into acting hastily, and try to take Zamora out of the equation."

"I agree with Excalibur," states Sylvia. "Protecting Czar and the artifacts should be our number one concern. Sidewinder can and will be dealt with, and Rock doesn't have to know that I was involved."

"I know that you're right," states Marquise, "However, these new developments are not sitting well with me at the moment. But I am willing to hear you out Sylvia."

Still stunned by all she has just heard, Zamora remains quiet and that concerns the other three. However, they will have to deal with her silence later. Right now they need to make some decisions, and they need to be the right decisions.

Sylvia begins to outline her plans on how they should proceed. "I will need to know every detail of the plans currently in place from the time the artifacts touch ground in Dakar to the time they are turned over to the museum. I need to know the names of every person involved with the case from top to bottom, and I will make sure that nothing happens to the artifacts before they can be secured inside the museum."

"Erik and Marquise, it will be your job to make sure that no harm comes to Zamora. And you might want to let Swamp Rat and Cockroach know about the latest developments as they will be critical to the plan's success."

"Once I have the details about the artifacts and everyone involved, I will come up with a plan to protect the artifacts and dispose of anyone not on our side. Once my plans are put into place, I will let you know what they are, so that you can be prepared for whatever happens."

Sylvia pauses before making her next statement, "Once my plans are in place, you will not see me again. You will not even know when I have left the country."

Understanding the need for her to remain a ghost, Marquise and Erik simply nod. Zamora still has not spoken, and all three turn in her direction.

"I'm fine. I just needed to organize some things in my head," Zamora states. "I think that you all should know that I will do my part in making this mission a success, while at the same time making sure that I stay alive."

Grateful that she is on board, Marquise walks over to her and gives her a quick hug before sitting down with Sylvia and giving her all the information that has requested. Once that is complete, Marquise, Erik, and Zamora make their way back to the hotel.

134

Heart Body and Soul

Needing time to process the latest developments of the case, Zamora heads to her room to take a long relaxing bath and to think.

Erik goes into his room and places the call to GL.

"What's up E&J," asks GL when he answers his phone.

"New wrinkle in the plan."

"Who?"

"Sidewinder."

"What," yells GL into the phone.

"Relax," responds E&J, "We have a new player on our side, but they must remain a ghost if we are to succeed."

"Come to the suite."

"Be right over."

Marquise contacts Cockroach to let him know of the latest developments in the mission.

"Cockroach."

"Pathfinder here."

"New path?"

"New player." When Cockroach doesn't respond, Marquise continues, "She's living up to her name, Snake Chaser overheard a conversation between Sidewinder and King Gamboto in the museum curator's office."

"Never did like that slippery son of a bitch," hisses Cockroach. "What's the plan?"

"Snake Chaser will handle the take down. You'll handle the disposal," answers Marquise. "Rock can never know."

"Don't think he would have a problem with it if he did."

"Just trying to keep the circle intimate."

"Roger that." They disconnect the call.

Erik and Marquise emerge from their rooms just as there is a knock on the door. "GL", states Erik when Marquise looks in his direction. Marquise lets out a sigh of relief that they wouldn't have to do battle at the moment.

Erik opens the door so that GL can enter the suite. The three of them take a seat around the coffee table, and Erik is first to speak, "Sidewinder is apparently making a side deal with the museum curator and the head of the Gamboto tribe for the artifacts," he begins. "However, he doesn't know that we are on to him or that we have a ghost player on our team."

"How did you come by this information," asks GL followed by a second question, "and who is this ghost?"

"The information was supplied by the ghost whom you know as Snake Chaser," responds Erik.

GL raises his eyebrows in surprise at this revelation. "I assume you called her in," GL asks of Marquise.

"Actually I called her in," responds Erik.

"You," asks GL in surprise. "How the hell do you know Snake Chaser?"

"She helped get me off the streets of DC as a teen, and helped me get on with the agency, anonymously of course," is Erik's answer.

136

With his mind a little twisted by the information he's just received, GL says, "Start from the beginning on how Snake Chaser came to be here, and how she found out about Sidewinder being a true snake."

Since his mind is on Zamora, Marquise lets Erik fill GL in on the latest developments of their mission, and their plans to deal with E-Dub. Just as Erik is giving the last details about their plans, Zamora walks into the living area and takes a seat. Marquise gives her his full attention, and can tell that she just wants to listen for the moment so he lets her be.

"Cockroach is here too," asks GL.

"Yes," answers Marquise, "I called him in when we first arrived and the villagers thought that Zamora was Princess Zahara." He turns to Zamora when he states her real name to gauge her reaction. She gives no indication that she's affected by hearing her true name.

"So what is my role to be when this plan unfolds," asks GL.

"You will be responsible for getting Czar to safety if things don't go as planned," responds Marquise.

Full Disclosure

"Since I am to be present for the authentication process at the museum that shouldn't be a problem," responds GL.

"There is another wrinkle in our plans," states Marquise as he pulls his phone out of his pocket. He brings up the pictures of the Americans that are suspected of black market art deals, and hands the phone to GL as he explains who they are, "These are faces of Americans suspected of selling African art on the black market," he begins, "However, we are not sure if they are 5 different people or one person with multiple disguises," he continues. "So you will have to keep a watchful eye out for them, as well as, E-Dub, the Gambotos, and Monsieur Orogotto," he concludes.

"There are beginning to be too many players on this field," states GL while studying the photos.

"I agree," states Marquise. "I will send the photos to your phone so that you may study them at length later."

"Thanks," states GL as he hands Marquise back his phone.

"Since you were not present at the last debriefing, there is another piece of information that you need to know about," begins Erik.

"What would that be," asks GL.

Heart Body and Soul

"Zamora really is the missing Princess Zahara."

GL sinks back against the couch cushions as he processes that bit of information. "Seriously?"

"Seriously," Zamora speaks for the first time since entering the room. All eyes turn her way. "I managed to get through the rest of the tapes that I found in my parent's belongings, and the last tape was a recorded message to me," she pauses as she fights to quell the butterflies in her stomach. "They told me about the plans the King and Queen made to get me and the royal artifacts out of the country, and that it was planned by the King and Queen that they return and reclaim the kingdom before my 30th birthday." She takes several deep breaths before continuing, "Apparently, I, as rightful heir to the throne, must claim the throne, marry, and give birth to the next line of our family before I turn 30, or the kingdom could be fought for and surrendered to the winner."

Stunned by this revelation, the three men in the room simply stare at her with their mouth's hanging open. As the reality of her situation sinks in, silent tears run down Zamora's cheeks, and she begins trembling with silent sobs. This sets Marquise into action. He practically runs to her, and gathers her in his arms. "Shh Sweetheart," he whispers over and over in her ear. "It's going to be alright," he adds.

Zamora snaps her head up, and tries to disengage herself from his arms to no avail. So, she practically yells at him through her sobs, "How is everything . . . going to be . . . alright! I'm already 28!! This means I . . . have to get married . . . and give birth in . . . less than two years!!!" She then begins sobbing in earnest, and Marquise tries to gather her closer to him but she begins pushing out his arms again. When he doesn't let her go, her anger gets the best of her, "I can't . . . imagine giving . . . birth to anyone's child . . . but yours," she yells at him.

Marquise closes his eyes, as he can't imagine her giving birth to anyone's child but his as well. However, he knows in his heart that can never be.

As that reality hits him he drops his arms to his side as he says, "We both know that I can't be your child's father." He then turns to walk away.

Zamora's sobs are instantly forgotten, and rage takes over. She grabs him by the arm and spins him in her direction, "Don't you . . . understand that I . . . love you," she yells at him. "I could never . . . let another man touch me . . . the way that you have!"

Marquise grabs both of her arms, "I love you too Czar," he yells back at her. "And as much as I want to claim you as mine forever, I can't! Why can't you understand that?"

Not wanting to back down, especially since he has revealed that he loves her in return, she frames his face with her hands and calmly states, "But you have claimed me. Heart, body, and soul."

Her words are Marquise's undoing, and he gathers her in his arms and kisses her for all she's worth. Feeling as though the couple needs time alone, Erik and GL leave the suite for the lounge of the hotel.

Once the need to breathe takes over, they break off the kiss and simply stand there staring into each other's eyes for what seems like an eternity. Finally it hits Marquise that they are not alone, and he turns in the direction of his fellow agents only to find that they have left the suite. "Shit," he hisses, but before he can say anything more Zamora kisses him. After a few moments of enjoying the taste of her lips, he breaks off the kiss, "Baby," he begins before kissing her nose, "You laid claim to my heart, body, and soul two years ago in Georgia." The tears begin running down her face in earnest again at his words. He kisses the tears from her cheeks before saying, "I hope those are tears of joy." She smiles, and he smiles as well before kissing her breathless once again. Once he catches his breath again, he frames her face in his hands before saying, "The last thing I want is for another man to kiss you, touch you, make love to you." He pauses and takes a deep breath before continuing, "But you're an African Princess, and I'm an American. The people of this country would not accept me as your husband."

She places her hands over his, "If you're the man I choose, they will have no choice but to accept you," she responds.

"It's not that simple," he counters.

"Yes it is! I could never let another man kiss me, touch me, make love to me."

He closes his eyes at her words wishing she would stop saying them, but his feelings overwhelm him and he picks her up in his arms and takes her to his bed. He all but rips her clothes from her before disposing of his own. Fueled by pure desire, he buries himself deeply inside her womanly core pausing only long enough for her to adjust to his size before making love to her in earnest. Their shouts of completion echo throughout the room, and then they promptly fall asleep spent from all the emotions they have just gone through in a short amount of time.

*****

Once they are seated at a table with drinks in their hands, GL asks, "What am I missing?" Knowing just what he means, E&J tells GL what he knows of the relationship between Zamora and Marquise. "Wow," is all GL can say at first. "This is certainly an unexpected development," he adds. "Their relationship is not going to jeopardize the mission, is it?"

"It hasn't so far," responds E&J before taking another sip from his glass. "However, this latest development has me asking the same question. I just hope that if Zamora is placed in harm's way that Marquise doesn't lose his cool, and does something that could jeopardize both of their lives and ours."

"I agree with you there," states GL as he drains his glass before signaling for the waitress.

An hour later, GL announces that he's going to head back to his hotel room, so both gentlemen leave the lounge for their respective beds.

141

ReGina Crawford

Silent Preparations

Unaware that he has been seen meeting with the enemy, E-Dub continues his preparations for getting his hands on the artifacts so that he may sell them to Orogotto. He schedules a meeting with the forger to make sure that the paperwork will stand up to scrutiny by the governments of both countries, for the paperwork is crucial to his plan.

As he arrives at the building being used by the forger, the hairs on the back of his neck stand up. He scours the surrounding area looking for unwanted visitors, but sees no one. He continues his walk to the back door of the building still feeling a little uneasy, and as he raises his hand to knock, takes one more look over his shoulder. Still seeing no one, he knocks and enters the building once the door has been opened.

Sylvia, true to her name of Snake Chaser, is watching his every move from her camouflaged location only fifty feet from the door. Knowing that E-Dub would need the best paperwork to pull off any type of coup, she has been staking out the forger's place for the past two days as he is the best in this part of the world. Knowing she can't anticipate his every movement, she places a tracking device on E-Dubs car once he enters the building. She then pulls out a small parabolic microphone to hear what is taking place inside the building.

Once inside the building, E-Dub questions the forger, "How is your surveillance around this place?"

"I assure you that my surveillance is top notch," he replies in an agitated voice. "No one could get within 200 feet of this place without me knowing about it!"

"Are you sure? I could have sworn I felt someone watching me as I walked up to the door."

"Paranoid much," asks the forger. "I can show you the footage from the cameras for the last five days," he continues. "You would then see that no one has been near this place except for me."

"Fine! Show me the paperwork," states E-Dub still feeling a little uneasy.

The forger unlocks a file cabinet, and pulls out the paperwork in question. "Look it over," he states while handing the papers over. "You will find that they are flawless, and will pass any scrutiny by any authenticator in the world. I would not have been able to stay in business as long as I have if I was not the best at what I do. Even your government has solicited my services a time or two."

"Oh shut up and let me look them over," states an aggravated E-Dub. He pulls out a small magnifying glass so that he may look at the intricate details of the documents. Half an hour later, E-Dub has completed his review of the documents, and is satisfied that they indeed look authenticate. He hands the forger an envelope containing his payment, and places the documents inside his coat. "It was nice doing business with you," states E-Dub as he takes his leave.

Once again the hairs rise on the back of his neck as he walks back to his car. He again scours the country side, and still sees nothing amiss. "I'll be glad when this is all over," he mumbles to himself. "I've never been this paranoid in my life. This just goes to prove it's time for me to get out of the spy business." He gets in his car and drives away.

Sylvia waits thirty minutes after E-Dub has driven away before approaching the door of the forger, and knocking. He opens the door
144

expecting to find the ungrateful American standing there, and is stunned to find a woman at his door holding two large guns on him. "Shut up and walk backwards slowly," she hisses before he can say a word.

He does as he's told, and she kicks the door closed behind her. Once inside, she holsters her weapons before laughing at the frown on the man's face. "Come on Ivan," she states. "Loosen up a little."

"Little girl, I should thrash you," he states. He then bursts out laughing and gathers her in a big bear hug. "What are you doing here?"

She hugs him in return before responding, "It seems the gentleman who just left here is trying to bring harm to a friend of mine, and I just cannot allow that to happen."

"So he was right. There was someone watching him," states Ivan the forger. "You're ability to show up undetected still amazes me," he adds. He shakes his head before asking, "Who are you protecting now?"

"Someone I've been protecting for many years . . . Zahara."

Stunned by the revelation that the princess is still alive, Ivan is rendered speechless for several moments. "She's still alive," he asks his voice barely above a whisper.

"Yes, she's still alive. And she is in possession of the royal artifacts that the American is trying to steal and sell to Orogotto."

"Damn," he hisses. "I assumed he got his hands on the artifacts after that couple was killed two years ago. I never dreamed that Zahara was still alive and now in possession of them."

"It's okay, dear friend. No one was to know that she was alive, and I have made sure that her identity has been kept secret all these years. Even when she traveled to this country two years ago after the death of the Richardsons."

"So what's your plan now that he has the documents that show him to be the rightful owner of the artifacts?"

"What I need to know is where you camouflaged your signature on the documents," she responds. At his stunned silence, she continues, "I know that you sign every document that you make, and since time will be of the essence when I take him down I need to know where it is as I will not have time to search for it myself."

"How . . . How do you know that," he asks.

"I have studied your documents for years, and it was only two years ago that I discovered your distinct signature in one of the documents. After I discovered it, I looked over every document you have made that I could get my hands on, and discovered that you put the same signature on every document that you make. Now, tell me where I can find the signature on the documents you just handed over."

"You are so lucky that I love you Sylvia, otherwise this meeting would not have a happy ending for you."

She throws her head back and laughs, before saying, "All of your weapons have been disabled, Ivan. You couldn't do me in if you wanted to."

He shakes his head and gives her the information she has requested. They give each other a giant bear hug, and she takes her leave.

The Wait

Zamora, Marquise, E&J, and GL are impatiently waiting on the artifacts to finally arrive. Due to the number of players in the game, they decide that it's best to stay out of public as much as possible. Marquise, E&J, and GL have been spending most of their time checking and rechecking the plan of action they plan to take the day the artifacts arrive. They need to make sure that they have no areas of exposure along the route from customs to the museum, as well as, inside the museum since they have no idea when anyone plans to make a move on the artifacts or Czar.

Czar has been keeping to herself as her emotions are highly charged, and being near Marquise after he has made it clear that he will return to America has been too painful for her. She knows that she has to maintain her focus if she is to come out this alive, and when he's near her the only thing that she can focus on is him.

Just as they are about to break for the afternoon, they receive a call from the front desk that a message has been left for them. Unsure who or what could be waiting for them down in the lobby, E&J and GL take separate paths to the lobby while Marquise stays in the suite with Zamora who is in her room unaware of the current events. GL enters the lobby from the stairwell on the opposite side of the lobby from the elevators just before the elevators open and E&J steps into the lobby. GL calls E&J's cell phone just as he steps off the elevator to give him a reason to pause and check his surroundings before approaching the desk. E&J is on the phone less than ten seconds before he spots Sylvia in the far corner of the lobby, and lets GL know that the message is legit. He hangs up the phone and approaches the front desk to retrieve the message. Once he places the message in his jacket pocket, he returns to the elevators to go back to the suite. Just as the doors open, he turns back to see that Sylvia has left her post in the lobby. GL makes his way back to the suite the same way he came, and meets E&J at the door to the suite. They enter the suite to find Marquise on the sofa just staring at the door to Zamora's bedroom. They know that he heard them enter the suite, but he never removes his eyes from her door. They take the seats they vacated to go retrieve the message, and simply wait for M&M to acknowledge their presence. It's five minutes later before he breaks eye contact with door and turns to them.

"Where's the message," he asks.

E&J retrieves the message from his jacket pocket, and hands it over as he states, "I believe it's from Snake Chaser as she was in the lobby when I stepped off the elevator."

Marquise simply nods as he opens the envelope. He begins to read the message out loud, "When the forged papers are presented, there will be the picture of a phoenix in the dot above the third I on every page. This is the forger's signature."

Marquise and GL speak at the same time, "Micro dots."

"Even with as long as I've known her, I'm still amazed at her ability to gain information that no one else is able to get," adds Marquise.

"She is very crafty," adds GL.

"That's why I called her in," states E&J. "She was able to find out my next move even before I knew what my next move was going to be." He pauses as he remembers his first encounters with Sylvia. "I can't tell you the number of times she saved my life on the streets of DC."

148

"You know," begins Marquise, "with this bit of information we could let the thieves steal the artifacts, and then bust them at the sale."

"I don't know about that," states E&J. "That could definitely increase the risk of the mission as the thieves may go ahead and give the kill order for Czar once they get their hands on the artifacts, since without her around the artifacts would be up for grabs even if the forgery is brought to light."

"Lot of wisdom from the young'un in that statement," comments GL.

Marquise sighs. "I know. I know. I just don't want her," he states as his eyes move to Zamora's bedroom door, "leaving this suite until this is all over."

"You know she would not sit still for that," states GL. "This mission is way too important to her in more ways than one, and from what I've heard about her, she never backs down in the face of danger."

"Yeah, she's a lot like Sylvia in that way," adds E&J.

"I know," he says again as he continues to stare at the door.

"Why don't you just go in there instead of staring at that damn door," asks GL.

"Because I'm not in control of my emotions around her," he begins. "And I don't want her to force a promise from me that I won't be able to keep."

"If I knew my time was limited with the woman that I loved above all others, I would spend every precious second I could with her," states GL.

Marquise doesn't respond. He just sits there staring at the door. Suddenly he stands up and takes long purposeful strides to the door to Zamora's bedroom.

E&J looks at GL, and states, "I think we should make ourselves scarce right about now." GL merely nods before getting on his feet and heading to the front door of the suite with E&J right on his heels.

Marquise doesn't bother to knock on the door, he simply strolls right into the room. However, he stops dead in his tracks when he finds the room empty and a note in the middle of the bed.

> *Sorry My Love.*
> *This waiting was driving me crazy,*
> *and I need some answers I can only find*
> *out from my people. I promise to be careful.*
> *Love Czar*

The anger he feels at reading her words forces a fierce growl to erupt from his throat. He immediately sends out an SOS to Erik, Giovanni, Rock, and Sylvia. As he waits for GL and E&J to return to the suite, he contacts Cockroach to let him know they need to find the missing princess and fast.

"Cockroach."

"Pathfinder here."

"Eyes on her."

"Seriously?"

"Yes. I've been watching the hotel for a couple of days now. Saw her when she ducked out of the service entrance of the hotel. Great disguise she's wearing too. I almost missed her. To keep her safe, it's best if you and your team stay put."

Pissed that she left the hotel but more concerned for her safety, Marquise agrees and disconnects the call. He cancels the SOS to everyone just as GL and E&J enter the suite.

"What the hell is going on," asks Erik. Marquise hands over Zamora's note. After reading the note he passes it on to GL before asking, "So why did you cancel the SOS if she's left the suite?"

"Cockroach has her in his sight," is Marquise's response. "He thinks it's best if we stay put so that no one finds out that she has left the hotel."

GL, who has just finished reading the note, states, "He's right. If the people who are after her see use tearing out of here without her in tow, they'll know she's out there without the benefit of bodyguards."

At that moment, Erik gets a buzz from Sylvia.

"Excalibur."

"She's safe. Cockroach and I have eyes on her."

"We know. Cockroach already informed Pathfinder. We're staying put. You guys just make sure she returns safely."

"Will do, young'un."

He hears her laughter just as she disconnects the line. "Sylvia's on top of her as well," he states to the room before he takes a seat. "I guess there's nothing for us to do but wait for her to return."

Marquise is beside himself even though he knows she's safe with Cockroach and Snake Chaser watching her back, so he heads to the mini-bar and downs a bottle of scotch and then a second one. After the liquor settles in his stomach, he states, more to himself than the others, "I should have gone in that room sooner."

"You had no way of knowing that she would try something like this," states GL, "None of us did."

"That doesn't matter," he practically yells as he opens up yet another bottle of scotch. "I still shouldn't have stayed away from her this long," he states before draining the third bottle.

"Take it easy there with the scotch," states GL. At Marquise's glare, he throws his hands in air to say he's backing off. However, he turns to E&J for help who promptly shakes his head no to indicate he's not saying a word.

Marquise downs one more bottle before heading to his room to work off his frustration with the whole situation.

Answers

The waiting is driving Zamora crazy, and not being around Marquise is not helping her state of mind. She has gone over and over in her head how she would like things to go between them, but she knows he's going to fight her every step of the way if she can't assure him that he would be accepted as her mate. She has to come up with a plan to make him her husband and the father of her children, but she's not sure how to make that happen. Then it occurs to her that they only people who can help her are her people. So she comes up with a plan to get out of the hotel, and visit the people of her kingdom.

She dresses up in the native dress of the villagers, and not the same type of garb that she wore while meeting with the monsieur, and makes her way out of her room via the laundry chute in her bathroom. From the laundry area she exits the hotel via the service entrance, and heads to the outskirts of the village. Her kingdom is not far and in an attempt to not draw attention to herself, she walks the distance.

Upon her arrival, she searches out the Xaliifa, the religious leader of the kingdom for he should be able to provide her with the answers she seeks. Having studied up on the region after her parent's death and before returning on this mission, she knows exactly where to find him.

Once she reaches him, she asks for private council for she is faced with a great dilemma and needs guidance. Once they reach his private chambers, she removes her head rap to reveal her face.

The Xaliifa gasps as he recognizes her as Princess Zahara. He recovers quickly and immediately bows down to her, "Your Grace," he states.

"Shhhhh," is Zamora response. "No one must know that I am here."

"Yes, yes. I understand," he responds. After a few deep breaths to calm himself, he asks, "What are you doing here? And why are you dressed so?"

"I come seeking answers, and no one must know of my presence until those trying to kill me are caught."

"Ah, yes. I have heard of the threats against you made by the people of the Gamboto Kingdom. However, once you claim the throne, you will have twenty-four hour protection so you will have nothing to fear."

"I have to be sure of that," she states. "This kingdom has been without royal command for over twenty-eight years, and I need to know that the people would welcome my return."

"Of course they would child! They have been praying for your return since the death of the King and Queen. No one believed that you were with them at the time of their death. Most believe that you are being kept safe in another kingdom until you have been deemed ready to claim the throne."

"I have actually been living in America all these years, and only recently found out about my true identity. And that is what concerns me. Will the people of the kingdom accept me as their princess knowing that I have been immersed in American Culture and the not the culture of this land?"

154

"That may present a problem, however, I believe that most will be able to overlook that fact if it means that we will no longer have to fear being overtaken by the Gambotos."

"That is another of my concerns. Will the Gambotos double their efforts to do away with me after I accept the throne? I do not wish to live my life in constant fear."

"Child you will be surrounded by loyal guards twenty-four hours, and no harm will come to you. Of this I am certain. Your parent's royal guard has remained loyal to them all these years, and have handpicked and groomed the current guard. They will be loyal servants."

"I am glad to hear that. Can you explain to me the importance of the Royal Artifacts that were also smuggled to America with me?"

"So it is true? The artifacts are safe?"

"Yes, the artifacts are safe, and are scheduled to arrive in four days time. However, there are people out there intent on stealing them, and selling them on the black market to the highest bidder. Who at present appears to be the curator of the IFAN museum."

"Orogotto. Yes, he has never gotten over the fact that he was banned from the kingdom, and not allowed to assume the throne after the death of the King and Queen. The artifacts must remain in your possession at all costs, for without them your position as the Princess will be challenged at every opportunity possible."

"There is still one more thing that concerns me."

"What is that child?"

"According to a recording left for me by my parents, I am to marry and give birth to the first heir to the throne by the time of my 30th birthday."

"That is true based on our tradition of a female assuming the throne. I assure you that we will be able to find you a suitable mate as soon as you as you assume your role as Princess."

"That is my concern. I have fallen in love," her voice trails off and she drops her eyes.

"And whom is this man you profess to love?"

"He is an American," she states as she raises her eyes to his once again. "He is already very loyal to me, and I know that he loves me with all of his heart."

"Then the problem lies where, child?"

"He does not believe that the people of the kingdom will accept him as my mate, and he is willing to walk away from me and return to America for my sake and the sake of the people of this kingdom."

"He does indeed seem very loyal to you if he is willing to live out the remainder of his days with a broken heart. I assure you that once he has proven his loyalty to you and the people of the kingdom, he will be freely accepted by all."

"How can you be so certain?"

"You do not know?"

"Know what?"

"Your father, the King was not of African or royal descent when he married your mother, yet the people of this kingdom loved him as though he was one of us."

"Really?"

"Yes child, really."

156

"Thank you Xaliifa, you have helped me a great deal. Now you must not tell anyone of my visit, or that I am even in this country. Until the artifacts arrive and the assassins and thieves are caught, my life shall remain in danger."

"Your secret is safe with me."

"Thank you again. Now I must return to the hotel before I place myself in more danger than I already have by coming here."

"Safe travels Princess."

Feeling as if a great weight has been lifted off of her shoulders, Zamora makes her way out of the kingdom, and heads back to the hotel. She is sure that she will be in big trouble once she returns to the hotel, but she is not concerned about it. She has the answers she needs to bind Marquise to her always, and that is all that matters at this moment.

Unbeknownst to her, Sylvia and Cockroach are assuring her safe travel back to the hotel for there have been eyes watching her since her arrival in the kingdom. Cockroach lets Marquise know when she is almost at the hotel so that he can assure that she makes it back to the suite unharmed. Marquise assumes she will return to her room the same way that she left, so he clears the laundry facility to await her arrival.

ReGina Crawford

Sealed with a Kiss

As Zamora approaches the hotel, her nerves get the better of her as she wonders if anyone has noticed that she's not in her room. However, she decides that the information she received is worth any backlash she'll receive from her fellow agents, including Marquise. She slips back in through the service entrance, and makes her way to the laundry facilities. It's quiet. Almost too quiet, and this makes her a little apprehensive. She calmly walks around the room to see if she can discover why there is no activity taking place when out of the shadows a body appears. She shows no fear, and readies her body for battle for she'll be damned if she'll go quietly.

"Relax Czar," whispers the voice from the lone figure. "It's only me, and I have no desire to thrash you in public."

Her heart sinks and then pounds furiously in her chest as she recognizes the voice. "So you discovered I was not in my room," she states.

"Yes I did, and I can't believe you would be so stupid as to pull a stunt like this."

"I am not stupid," she practically yells. "I am a highly trained agent, and can handle myself well in any situation."

"Not this one, but I won't discuss this further with you right here. Let's go back to the room, and then we'll finish our conversation about your stupidity."

"Fine," she states heatedly and heads in the direction the servants use to enter the hotel lobby.

He grabs her arm, as he states, "Uhn't uh. Let's go back the way you planned if you hadn't been discovered."

"No problem," she states wanting to smack the smug smile off his face. Not willing to let him get the upper hand, she walks over to the laundry chute and begins her climb back up to her room. It's a grueling climb, and knowing that Marquise is right underneath her is making it that much harder.

What she doesn't know is that he's regretting his decision almost as much as she is at the moment. The heated scent of her body is playing havoc on his senses as it drifts down to him during their climb. He's trying to ignore it, for he knows that it's dissolving his anger with each breath he inhales, but it's damn near impossible for him not to be affected by it. He's become addicted to her smell, her taste, her touch. His thoughts anger him since he knows he can't have her for a lifetime, and he angrily whispers, "Can you move a little faster? I'm cramped in here."

She continues to climb at the same pace as she mumbles, "Nobody told you to play super hero and come down here. Trying to rush me when this was his idea. He should have went first if he wanted to set the pace."

"What was that," he asks.

"What was what?"

"Never mind, just climb."

Zamora finally reaches her room, pulls open the chute, and rolls into her bathroom. She's exhausted, and doesn't move for a minute thinking she has time before Marquise gets to the chute. However, she was wrong as he tumbles out on top of her a few seconds later. She temporarily loses her breath at the impact, and is unable to speak at first. Then she feels the heat of his body through her clothes, and is at a loss for words. But she can act, and she does. She kisses him with all that she is, and he is powerless to resist the force of her kiss so he kisses her in return.

Marquise regains control of his senses first, and pins her hands above her head. "No you don't," he says while trying to control his breathing. "I will not be distracted by your honey filled kisses. I am extremely pissed at you, and I will have my say."

"Honey filled kisses, huh," she says around a smile.

Her smile is infectious and he smiles back at her, but is not distracted from his anger at her. "Nice try sweetheart, but I won't be sidetracked again," he states as he sits up pulling her with him as he has yet to release her wrists. He then stands up, and pulls her with him. Once they are on their feet, he marches her into her bedroom, and sits her on the bed before pulling up a chair directly in front of her. "You know what you did tonight was extremely stupid and dangerous," he begins. "You were extremely lucky that you made it back here in one piece," he continues. "What the hell were you thinking," he yells at her

"It was not stupid," she yells in return, "and I was extremely careful! No one even saw me, so how much danger could I have been in?"

"It was stupid," he yells, "And you were seen! How do you think I knew when you would be entering the hotel?" Stunned by what he has just said, Zamora is silent. "The thought never crossed you mind that I was waiting for you and that's why the laundry facility was empty, did it?"

"No," she whispers.

"You have no idea the danger you placed yourself in!"

160

"What I did was necessary and I would do it again if it brought me the answers I was seeking."

Now it's Marquise's turn to be stunned into silence. "What answers," he asks when she continues to remain silent as well.

"I needed to know what my life would be like in this country if I stayed, and took the throne."

"What do you mean if?"

"I don't think that I can marry a man I don't know and who I don't love. I needed to know how the people of my kingdom would feel about the man who has claimed my heart."

"Zamora, we've talked about this. The decision has been made. You will assume your rightful place on the throne, and I will return to America."

"You decided that," she all but screams as she stands up. "I never agreed to any of that, and I won't agree to that!"

"You don't have a choice, sweetheart."

"I do have a choice, and I choose you!" She begins pacing the room in her anger for it seems he is determined to leave her with a broken heart and a lost soul. She stops directly in front of him, "I can't live without you," she calmly states. "And I don't have to. The answers that the Xaliifa gave me have helped me make my decision. The rest is up to you."

"Zamora, what are you talking about? What answers did the Xaliifa give you?"

She takes his hands in hers before speaking, "He told me that my father was not from this country, and that the people of the kingdom gladly accepted him once they realized how much my mother loved him and how much he loved her in return." She pauses to let him process that bit of information before continuing, "So you see, I don't have to live without

161

you. You don't have to go back to America taking my heart and soul with you."

He is silent for so long that Zamora starts to think that she has made a mistake after all, so she lets go of his hands. However, before she can take one step away from him, he stands and gathers to him and kisses her for all he's worth. The need for air is the only thing that separates his lips from hers. He rests his forehead against hers as he tries to catch his breath. "Sweetheart, are you sure?"

"Am I sure of what," she asks as she too tries to control her breathing.

"Are you sure that you want to spend the rest of your life with me? Bear my children?"

She frames his face in her hands, and says, "There is no one else that I want to wake up to in the morning. No one else that I want to hold me as I sleep. No one else who's likeness I want to see on the face of my children. You are my heart and soul," she states before laying claim to his lips.

Overjoyed by her answer, Marquise dives head first into the kiss conveying all the love he has for her through his lips.

Sidetracked

Deciding that the kiss is not nearly enough to convey her joy at being able to hold on to her man, Zamora runs her hand across all that makes him male. The sensation of her touch sends him soaring, and Marquise forgets about all that they need to discuss as he begins stripping her out of her clothing. As she stands there in all her natural glory, he removes his clothes before pulling her into the bathroom. He turns on the water for the shower before leading her inside. As the warm water cascades over them, Marquise runs his soap lathered hands all over her body making her moan with each caress. Once she's lathered to his satisfaction, he rinses her completely and is so mesmerized by the rivulets of water as they cascade down her body that he causes ripples in streams with his tongue. Loving the feel of her skin on his tongue, he continues running his tongue over her breasts, stomach, and thighs. The scent of her arousal causes his nostrils to flair, and he inhales deeply. He spreads her thighs wide and inserts his tongue deeply inside her womanly core, and inhales again. He gets on his knees, places her thighs on his shoulders, and presses her back against the shower wall as he feasts to his hearts delight. In no time at all she's grabbing the back of his head and screaming out his name as her climax crashes down on her with a force so strong it has her trembling.

Needing to be deep inside her, Marquise lowers her thighs to his waist as he stands up and enters her with one deep thrust. She wraps her thighs tight around his waist as he places his hands on the shower wall while thrusting continuously in and out of her. He kisses her, thrusting his tongue in her mouth the same way his manhood is thrusting inside her body. As his orgasm begins to crash down around him, she grinds her hips against him while squeezing her inner walls milking every ounce of fluid from him. Completely drained, he lowers her legs to the shower floor as his legs are trembling and he's not sure if he can hold his own weight let along both of theirs. Zamora reaches behind him and turns off the water before leading him to the bed where she lays him on his back. Even though his orgasm was intense, he is still standing at attention and she impels herself with all that makes him male. The upper half of his body jumps up off the bed at the feel of her gripping him in her silken sheath. She gentle pushes him back down with her hands on his chest before slowly raising her hips, and then sliding back down. She repeats the motion over and over as she savors every inch of him causing him to grip the sheets on the bed to prevent himself from flipping her on her back and riding her hard and fast. They stare into each other's eyes as she continues her slow ride mimicking the movements of a belly dancer. But soon the intensity builds to the breaking point, and Marquise flips them over, places her thighs over his shoulders and takes what he wants while giving her what she needs. They both scream out their release before he collapses on top of her unable to move a single muscle. She loves the feel of his spent body pressing her into the mattress, and closes her eyes as she basks in the afterglow of their loving.

It's thirty minutes before either of them move. Marquise rolls to his side pulling Zamora into his embrace. He places a finger under her chin so that he can look in her eyes. "You effectively sidetracked me from my anger at your leaving this suite, however, you still have a thrashing coming for that little maneuver," are his first words. He follows with, "But since I am currently too drained to give it to you, it'll have to wait and I won't be distracted again."

"Marquise, what harm was done by me leaving?"

"Cockroach and Sylvia saved you from harm, so we'll never know."

"What do you mean Cockroach and Sylvia saved me from harm," she asks breaking free of his embrace and sitting up on the bed.
164

"Apparently Sylvia knows you well, and has been keeping tabs on you. And when she isn't available, she enlists the help of Cockroach. They both followed you to your kingdom, and apprehended the band of rebels who followed you from your kingdom."

"What?"

"Yes, there was a group of three men following you when you left, and from what I understand their goal was to make sure you never made it back to the suite."

Zamora starts trembling as the reality of his words sink in for she never noticed anyone during her travels, and she is usually better than that. Marquise sits up and pulls her into his embrace to sooth her trembling. "I guess I was so lost in my own thoughts that I did not detect any danger during my travels," she begins. She turns to look him the eyes, "But I couldn't lose you. I just couldn't. I had to find out if there was a way for us to be together."

"While I understand what was driving you, it still was a foolish move on your part and you will promise me that you will not make such a move again." He sees the flash of defiance in her eyes, and before she can say a word he has her flat on her back and impels her with his manhood. "Promise me," he says in her ear while grinding his hips against her. "Promise me," he says again.

Unable to do anything but obey, Zamora barely gets out, "I promise," before lifting her hips off the bed offering him all of her. He grabs her hips in his hands, and thrusts deeply over and over until she is screaming his name in her release. He's right behind her with his own release, and she's screaming his name again as she feels his hot fluid fill her. Once again they both collapse on the bed completely drained. Sleep claims them both.

*****

165

As Marquise and Zamora emerge from her room the next morning, GL and E&J are sidetracked from their anger and her flight from the suite by the smiles on both of their faces. They turn and look at each other in confusion before E&J speaks up, "Please tell me that you did not let her off the hook for her little escapade last night?"

Marquise laughs before responding, "No, I did not let her off the hook." He looks her directly in the eyes before continuing, "And she has promised never to pull such a stunt again."

Never turning from his stare, she states, "I promise." He nods, and she nods in return.

E&J rolls his eyes at the two of them even though they are not aware of the gesture. "So what was the objective of this little trip you took?"

Before Czar could answer, E&J and Marquise receive SOS beeps on their phones.

Developments and Revelations

Marquise contacts Cockroach to find out what the SOS is all about, and at the same time E&J checks in with Sylvia. After they finish their conversations, they rejoin GL and Czar with angry looks on their faces.

"What is it," Zamora anxiously asks.

"It seems that your little escapade has forced someone's hand," Marquise answers first.

"What do you mean," Zamora asks more nervous than she was mere seconds ago.

"Orogotto has been killed and so has the museum greeter Sareena," bluntly states E&J. Marquise turns to him with more than a little anger in his face. "What? We don't have the luxury of being tactful at this point."

"I agree," interjects GL.

"I know you two are right," responds Marquise. "However, I don't think it's necessary to frighten Czar unnecessarily." It's at this point that everyone notices how silent and still she has become. Marquise grabs her hands, and notices how cold they feel. "Czar," he says her name barely above a whisper, and she continues to stand there with a frightened look on her face and unmoving. "Czar," he repeats a little louder. "Czar," he

167

growls while shaking her. She begins shaking on her own, and her knees buckle. "Whoa," he states as he takes her over to the sofa to sit down. "Breathe sweetheart, breathe," he states as he kneels before her. He begins rubbing her hands trying to warm them up as she tries to come to grips with what she has just heard.

E&J and GL are stunned by her reaction to the death of Orogotto. She has always exhibited such strength and courage throughout the mission, and to see her breakdown like this has left them at a loss for words.

"I'm sorry Czar," states E&J as he walks over to where she's sitting. "I wasn't trying to rattle you."

She looks up at him with fear in her eyes, and with a shaky voice states, "No need to apologize. I wasn't the bluntness of your statement that shook me, it's the ramifications of Orogotto's death that have me shook." She pauses and closes her eyes as she still tries to come to grips with this latest bit of news. They give her a little time to regroup and when she does, it's with the fierceness they are used to seeing from her. "Now that Orogotto is dead, E-Dub's plans are going to have to drastically change," she begins. "However, he is not going to want to reveal himself as the black market dealer, which will make him even more dangerous to this mission," she adds. "Rock may receive orders to pull out of the mission, however, we can't abandon the mission as my life depends on those artifacts making it back to this country," she continues. "So we may have to go rogue to see this through," she further adds as she looks at each one of them to see if they are on board with going rogue.

The three men are stunned by the instant transformation that takes place before their eyes, and are silent for a few minutes. E&J is the first one to speak, "Whoa, let's take a step back," he states as he feels she is being a little over dramatic.

"I agree," states GL.

"I say we hear her out," Marquise jumps in. The other two men look at him with sarcasm on their faces. Marquise holds up his hands in an effort to hold back their comments as he continues, "She may be right about E-Dub now that he's lost his buyer, he may decide to do something drastic to get the money he's after. And we already know that with her out of the way, her kingdom is up for grabs."

Realizing that he may be right, both me nod their heads in agreement. "Go ahead with your thoughts," states E&J.

"Everyone believes that the artifacts will not arrive in this country for another three days, so I say we move up the timeline," she states her thoughts out loud. "This way they won't have time to solidify their plans," she continues. "The artifacts can no longer go to the museum, so we will have to reveal my true identity."

"Whoa," interrupts Marquise. "I don't think that's such a good idea," he states. "That would be the equivalent of placing a price on your head."

"I'm aware of that," states Zamora, "However, the artifacts will require an owner, and at this point it will have to be me."

"No, it doesn't. There has to be another way that does not involve you placing yourself on the firing range," is Marquise's come back.

"She may be right," interjects GL who stands his ground when Marquise looks at him angrily. "If she doesn't come out as the princess and the rightful owner of the artifacts, there will most likely be a free-for-all brawl to gain possession of them. I don't think that any of us wants to be immersed in the middle of civil unrest in this country."

Marquise closes his eyes as he knows the words spoken by GL are true, and he knows he has to accept these new risks and threats to Zamora's life even though he doesn't want to. He opens his eyes before speaking, "I know that it has to be this way, however, I still don't like it. We will have to make sure that Czar's security is air tight, as well as, the security on the artifacts." He walks into his room only to return to the living area with his laptop. He sits down, opens it up, and immediately begins typing while speaking. "Alright, let's get this plan in motion," he begins. "I will

169

contact Cockroach to let him know that we will need is team in place sooner than originally planned. Excalibur, you will need to let Snake Chaser know what the new plans are for I'm sure her unique set of skills will definitely come in handy. GL, you will be responsible for finding out what information the embassy here has, and to prevent them from interfering with our plans. I suggest we change the cargo containers that the artifacts are being shipped in, so Czar you will need to contact the shipper and arrange that without tipping them off as to what our plans are since we don't know if any of them are involved in the plot to relieve you of the artifacts." Marquise pauses in his rattling off of instructions for everyone in the room.

Before he can speak again, Zamora quietly interjects, "The artifacts are already here." She then closes her eyes so that she is only peeking at them from one eye for she knows that the three men are about to start yelling. There is only silence for so long, that she opens both eyes and looks them all dead on. "Come on," she states, "Get it over with. I know that you're all ready to rip me a new one for keeping that bit of information from you."

"Actually, if I didn't think Marquise would rip my head off, I would kiss you right now," states GL. He laughs off the glare that he receives from Marquise.

Marquise quickly recovers from GL's comment, and turns to Zamora, "That is the best news you could have given us," states Marquise, "we can talk about the hows and whys of that later." Zamora is not fooled by the calm way he spoke, but lets him continue talking uninterrupted. "That eliminates one major risk for us, and will allow us to set up a sting operation to catch E-Dub in the act of trying to steal the artifacts when they arrive in country." He pauses as he reworks his plans in his head. "We should schedule a press conference at the US embassy to announce that Zamora is Princess Zahara," Marquise announces.

"Actually, I think the press conference should take place at the kingdom palace," counters Zamora. Before Marquise could get the first word out of his mouth, she holds up her hand to hold off his comments. "I know you think that it's best that we do this on American soil, but I think it will be more readily accepted if I announce who I am on African soil. That way the people of this country will see that I have already accepted the truth of my birth, and that I am ready to embrace this country as my own and take my rightful place as the Princess of Umboto."

"She has a valid point," states GL. At Marquise's angry glare, GL states, "You can quit glaring at me every time I agree with Czar. She and I have been doing this a lot longer than you have, and we are looking at this mission with seasoned eyes. You on the other hand are looking at this mission with a military eye, and unfortunately that's not helping with this mission. Our approach has to be more human in nature and less remote." He then turns to Zamora, "Please continue to tell us your ideas."

ReGina Crawford

Ad Lib

"The press conference should take place in the throne room at the palace, and the royal artifacts should be present in their normal display cases in the room," she pauses before making her next statement. "I think Marquise should be standing at my side as my chosen betrothed, and the next prince of the kingdom." She stops talking to gauge Marquise's reaction to what she just said, and he just stands there silent. She tries not to let her disappointment show as she continues on with the ad lib plans she has put together. "GL should also be at my side offering up the support of the American Government as the country adjusts to having a true royal leadership in place once again. Although Sylvia doesn't want the agency to know of her involvement, I believe we will need her on the perimeter to watch for snakes in the grass that we aren't aware of. Also, Cockroach and his crew will be needed for extra security, but they should let the Royal Guard take the lead as far as security goes. Is everyone okay with everything that I have laid out?"

"Exactly who am I," asks E&J.

"You will maintain your role as an art curator from America who has been overseeing the transport and care of the artifacts, and you will field any and all questions regarding the authenticity of the artifacts during the press conference," answers Zamora.

"How should we respond to questions about our arrival which the African people will surely see as a ruse," asks GL.

"The explanation for that will be that we needed to test the climate of the country. That we needed to be sure that there would not be political unrest due to my presence in the country. Along with that, that I needed to privately meet with the Xaliifa to receive his blessing on my choice for my mate."

"It seems that you have thought this through very thoroughly in such a short period of time," Marquise states rather suspiciously.

"My strength within the agency has been my ability to think on my feet in times of uncertainty," responds Zamora. "It has saved my life more times that I care to remember."

"I suggest we put this plan in motion, and rather quickly," states GL in an attempt to break the tension he feels building between Marquise and Zamora.

"I agree," states E&J. "I will contact Snake Chaser, and let her know of our plans and her role in them."

"I will contact Rock, set up the press conference, and get the Embassy staff up to speed," adds GL.

With everyone having their assignments, they depart the living area to carry out their tasks. Zamora goes to her room to regroup after the day's events. However, her well deserved moment of relaxation is short lived as Marquise enters her room a short ten minutes later. Although she's not surprised to see him, she freezes upon his entrance for she knows that the quiet before the storm is over.

"I don't know what question to ask first, so how about you just start from the beginning," he states as he takes a seat in the chair located on the opposite side of the room from her bed on which she is sitting partially undressed.

Determined not to be rattled by the anger she feels brewing just below the surface of his calm demeanor, Zamora crosses her arms under her scantily clad breasts effectively covering her bare stomach. "The artifacts were in the country even before we were," she begins. "Rock and I thought that it was best if no one but the two us knew that the artifacts were already in country just in case there was a government agent involved in the smuggling of art on the black market. And since E-Dub has been found out to be a major figure in the black market, I would say that that was a smart move on our part." She pauses and takes a deep breath before continuing, "The artifacts are actually being housed at the palace and have been since they arrived, so we were never worried about them being stolen. The negotiations with the museum were only a ruse to flush out the black market smugglers, and was obviously successful." She stops talking to see if Marquise has any questions about what she has just revealed, but he simply nods for her to continue.

"This was a perfectly planned mission until it was revealed that I was the missing princess. That was a completely unexpected revelation, and I must admit that it caught me completely off guard. I became unsure of what the outcome of the mission would be once that little tidbit was revealed. I'm left with a lot of unanswered questions." Becoming unnerved by his unwavering stare, Zamora gets up off the bed and grabs a T-shirt from one of her drawers to put on. "When you stated that you would return to the states and leave me here to assume the throne, I was lost," she reveals. "I didn't want to have to live without you, and needed to find a way for us to be together. Thus the reason I went to see the Xaliifa. I had to know that I wouldn't have to give you up, and marry some man I didn't know and could never love." Tired of the sound of her own voice, she stops talking and stares at him the same way he's staring at her.

"Please continue," is all that Marquise has to say.

"What else is there for me say?"

"Your plans for the press conference seemed rather detailed to be spur of the moment."

"I would love to take all the credit for that, however, I facilitated a similar press conference in a remote Chinese kingdom a few years ago on a mission of a similar nature. I simply modified the plans of that mission to fit the circumstances of this mission." Marquise tilts his head to the side at her last statement. "Yes, this is still a mission to me regardless of the fact that it is also my life. I wanted to make sure that my parent's deaths were indeed an accident, and that they weren't the victims of black market dealers who wanted to get their hands on the artifacts."

"Let's talk about your parents," begins Marquise. "Were they truly here at the wishes of the King and Queen, or was that a mission as well?"

"As far as I know, it was not a mission. Believe me, if it was, I would have definitely been here with them to ensure their safety."

Marquise continues to stare at here as he digests all that she has told him. Zamora begins pacing the room in his silence, but she remains quiet knowing that he has a lot of information to process. Once he has finished processing all that she's told him, he calls her name barely above a whisper. She stops pacing and faces him wondering when he stood up since she didn't notice the movement. "Come here," he says. She walks over to him stopping just short of being within arm's reach, afraid to get any closer. He crooks his finger at her beckoning her to come closer. She takes one more step in his direction and stops. He crooks his finger again as he says, "Come closer Zamora. I promise I won't bite you." She moves so that they are standing toe to toe, eye to eye. "Czar, I love you with all my heart and soul," he states as he gets down on one knee. Zamora's breath catches in her throat as she suspects that he's going to propose to her. "Will you join your life with mine, and be my friend, my lover, and the mother of my children?"

Zamora has to fight to breathe, but manages to find just enough air to say one word, "Yes."

Marquise pulls out a beautiful three carat pear-shaped orange diamond ring surrounded by twenty flawless white diamonds, and slips it on her finger. He can see by the way her mouth is hanging open that she is stunned. He stands up, puts a finger under her chin, and closes her mouth. She simply continues staring at the ring. He places his finger under her chin again, and raises her face to his. "It's the royal engagement ring."

"What? How?"

"After Sylvia dispatched the rebels that were following you after your visit to the Xaliifa, she paid the Xaliifa a visit. Apparently he was so moved by what you said, he asked her to bring me the ring for when I was ready to propose to you." Tears start rolling down her cheeks as a big smile forms on her lips. Marquise returns her smile before kissing the tears from her cheeks. "I take it you are pleased," he says in between kisses.

"I am very pleased," she states before cupping his face and kissing him fully. When she breaks the kiss, she takes one more look at the ring before saying, "I'm more than pleased."

He smiles before saying, "Not yet you're not, but you will be." He then strips them both before taking her to bed.

The Set Up II

The next morning they attend the meeting that Rock has called to discuss the latest developments with the entire team, including E-Dub. "There have been some unexpected developments in the case that require us to change our strategy," begins Rock.

However, before Rock can say another word, E-Dub interrupts him, "What developments? What kind of changes," he asks looking slightly nervous.

"If you'll let me continue, you'll find out," responds Rock with a scowl on his face. He takes a minute to regroup before speaking again. "As some of you know, Zamora has been mistaken for the missing Umboto Princess and an attempt to kill her was made. Also, there have been rumors that a heist is being planned to steal the artifacts on the day they are scheduled to arrive in this country, and now that Orogotto has been killed we can't afford to discount those rumors." He pauses and looks around the table so as not to give away the fact that he is closely watching E-Dub's reaction to his last statement. E-Dub remains calm as he is confident that no one in the room has a clue about his role in the heist. "As a result, we have decided to move up the arrival of the artifacts to tomorrow."

"How are we supposed to adjust our plans with less than 24 hours notice," asks E-Dub with more than a little agitation in his voice.

"Are you unsure of your abilities to adapt to this new schedule," asks Rock in as calm a voice as he can since he knows of E-Dub criminal plans.

Taken by surprise by the question and realizing the mistake he made in asking his question, E-Dub composes himself before replying, "I am more that capable of making the adjustment. I'm just concerned about the security surrounding the shipment. Do we have enough people in the country to deal with armed smugglers?"

"While we won't have the full security detail that was originally planned, I think we have enough people to handle the job effectively," is Rock's response. "May I continue, or do you have more questions?" E-Dub simply nods in Rock's direction that he may continue. "The original plan was for the artifacts to arrive by seaplane at the customs' dock, and now they will arrive by a charter plane at a private airstrip outside the Umboto Kingdom. The goal is to house the artifacts in a facility that is secure, and limit their exposure to the black market henchmen who plan on stealing them. Once they arrive at the airstrip, they will be secured in a vault in the palace so that they can be authenticated before being placed on display. And instead of authenticating all ten pieces, only the two major pieces will be authenticated. Once the authentication process is complete and the pieces are moved to their cases, there will be a press conference to inform the people of this country of their safe arrival and the plans to revive the legacy of the Umboto Kingdom."

"Just how are some pieces of art going to revive the Umboto legacy," E-Dub asks somewhat sarcastically.

"The art by itself will not revive the legacy, but we have been told that the Xaliifa of the kingdom has some news that will change the way the country is governed," is Rock's reply. E-Dub arches an eyebrow at that bit of information, and upon seeing that Rock asks, "You doubt the validity of the Xaliifa's words?"

"Not at all," responds E-Dub somewhat smugly, "I just don't believe that the people of the kingdom are going to embrace him as their leader if that's the announcement he plans to make." He pauses as he hears

178

movement at the other end of the table, so he takes a look at all of their faces before continuing, "I'm aware that the person who can show rightful ownership of the artifacts can claim the country's rule, but the Xaliifa is a man of the cloth and will not be able to effectively rule the country with the iron fist it will take to ward off anyone who wishes to take the country by force. Also, he will never produce heirs, so the country will be up for grabs once again after his death. Just doesn't seem logical to me, that's all I'm saying."

"Well since we don't know what the Xaliifa's announcement is at this time, I would say you are jumping the gun. However, let's table that discussion for now, and go over the timeline for tomorrow's events," states Rock as he hands out the typed timeline that he has put together.

They spend the next thirty minutes reviewing the timeline, and making sure everyone knows where they are supposed to be and when they are supposed to be there. "The timeline is tight," adds Rock, "so everyone must be in place at the time noted. So that no one jumps the gun too early, I have a synchronized watch for each of you," he continues as he slides a box down the table to each of them. "Each watch has been locked so there is no way anyone can tamper with the time, so make sure you have it on you at all times once you leave the compound." Everyone opens their box and swaps out the watch they are currently wearing. "If there is nothing else, good luck with your mission."

E-Dub is the first to leave the compound, however, he is unaware of shadow that is now following his every move. He gets in his car, and heads to his secret hideout to let his henchmen know of the change of plans. "I hope these monkeys can be ready tomorrow," he mumbles to himself as he drives. "I will get my hands on those artifacts, and I will get my money," he nearly yells as he pounds on the steering wheel. "I told Gamboto not to kill that damn curator! But did he listen? No!!! Now I've got to scramble to get my hands on those artifacts!" He instantly stops yelling as a thought enters his mind. *What if Gamboto is trying to double cross me as well? Could he have possibly known that with the curator killed the artifacts would then be sent to the Umboto Kingdom? Does he have plans to hijack the plane when it arrives at the airstrip?* "If that monkey thinks he's going to cut me out of this deal and cheat me out of my money, he better think again!"

*****

Once E-Dub has left the compound, Rock and the others go over their plans for the snatch and grab at the airstrip, as well as, their plans for the press conference.

"Cockroach and his men should be setting up their places at the airstrip as we speak," begins Marquise. "One of his men will serve as the pilot on the plane, and four of his men will serve as security on the plane with the artifacts," he continues. "There will also be eight men in hiding around the airstrip to handle whomever E-Dub has hired to hijack the artifacts," he concludes.

"I don't believe that he planned on being present for the theft of the artifacts in the beginning, but I wonder if our sudden change in plans will force him to show up at the airstrip," muses Rock out loud.

"I'm hoping it does," states GL. "It would make our jobs at the press conference a little easier."

"I guess we'll have to play it by ear tomorrow," states E&J. "If he calls to say he will be late to the press conference, then we'll know he plans to make a detour to the airstrip."

"As far as the press conference is concerned, we will have a small army battalion serving as security along with the Royal Guard from Umboto," begins Rock. "All of the journalist have been prescreened, and should arrive by this evening. The conference will be seen all over the world on every major news channel there is," he adds. "Czar, are you ready for that?"

"Do I have choice," she asks. At the odd looks she receives from her team members, she adds, "Yes, I'm ready. I've accepted the truth, and I am ready to assume my role as Princess." The team is still looking at her oddly and she knows what they are silently asking her, so she responds, "I've never had to face journalists in a setting of this magnitude, and I know that there will be plenty of questions about my life the past twenty-eight years, as well as, about the relationship between Marquise and I. I must admit that I am more than a little nervous about facing the press, but I know that it must be done."

Marquise takes her hand in his before saying, "I will be beside you the whole time holding your hand, so just squeeze mine whenever you feel overwhelmed. I will try to give you a few minutes reprieve by fielding some of their questions, okay?"

"Okay."

"I think we have done all we can today," Rock says. "I suggest we all get a good night's rest for tomorrow will be one hell of a day."

"Before we leave, I have an announcement to make," states Marquise. Rock doesn't say a word, he simply raises an eyebrow as he waits for Marquise to continue. "I have proposed to Zamora and she has accepted." Before he can say another word, the room erupts into a loud round of cheers and congratulations.

"I take it that means you're resigning from the agency," states Rock as he shakes Marquise's hand while hugging Zamora with his other arm.

"You are correct Sir," replies Marquise.

Rock then looks down at Zamora, and says, "It has been a pleasure working with you all these years, and I wish you the best on your new life journey, Princess."

"Thank you Sir," she responds, "This was not the outcome I expected when I took on this mission, but I am happy with results," she states as she looks over at her fiancée.

"The mission is not completely over yet, so get a good night's rest for tomorrow should prove to be very interesting," states Rock.

The four agents make their way back to their hotel to relax before the next day's fireworks.

The Takedown

While Czar and her crew are just getting up for the day, E-Dub is putting his plans in motion to hijack the artifacts the moment the plane touches ground. He was able to round up his band of criminals after leaving the compound yesterday, and they are in place waiting for his signal. Not trusting the Gambotos to not double cross him, he decides to go to the airstrip himself but remain out of sight. However, he is unaware that he has a mongoose on his tail, and she plans to capture the snake she's after.

Once she becomes aware of where Sidewinder is headed, Snake Chaser speeds ahead to the airstrip to take up her hiding place. She plans to let Cockroach and his men handle the thieves that E-Dub has hired, but she herself will take down Sidewinder.

E-Dub arrives at the airstrip, hides his car in a remote hanger, and then takes up his hiding place to await the aircraft. He has already received word that his band of thieves are already in place, and that they have not seen a single person in the vicinity since their arrival in the middle of the night. Little do they know that they were not the first people to arrive, and that there is a band of military personnel waiting to take them down the moment they move on the plane.

*****

Czar is packing her attire for the press conference when she hears a knock at her door. She tells the knocker to come in for she knows that it's no one other than Marquise. He enters the room and closes the door behind him before leaning against it, and she turns to him and smiles. "Good Morning."

"Good Morning Princess."

She stills her movements before replying, "That is still hard for me to hear."

"I suggest you get use to hearing it starting today. The people of your kingdom are going to be so happy to see you that there will probably be a steady stream of them in and out of the palace for quite a while."

"I know. It still takes me by surprise when I hear it though."

Seeing that she is a little shaky, Marquise walks over to her, and pulls her into his arms. She melts into him needing to release some of the tension that she is feeling over the day's events. He whispers in her ear, "Remember, I will be by your side the whole time, holding your hand. If you need to, pull strength from my presence." She nods her head as it lays on his chest. He kisses the top of her head, and holds her a few moments longer. "You need to finish packing," he states as he pulls back from their embrace. "We leave for the palace in about an hour."

Knowing that he is right, she doesn't protest the loss of his embrace and simply responds, "I'll be ready."

Marquise turns and leaves the room. He is greeted by E&J and GL in the living area. "How's she holding up," asks GL.

"She's putting on a brave face, but I know that she is a little nervous about the press conference."

"How are you doing," asks E&J.

"I must admit that this is a little nerve racking for me as well. I never thought that I would find a woman who could capture my heart and soul, and never dreamed that she would be a princess and that I would one day become her prince."

"Yeah, that is a lot to fathom," replies E&J.

"I agree," responds GL. "Has anyone heard from E-Dub this morning?"

"No," answers E&J, "but I did hear from Snake Chaser this morning, and he's at the airstrip."

"Afraid of being double crossed is he," snickers GL.

"Something like that," says E&J.

"I wonder if we'll get a chance to question him when this is all over," asks GL.

"I highly doubt it," replies E&J. "If I know Snake Chaser, he'll be taking his last breath sometime later today."

"The boy has a point," states Marquise.

*****

Meanwhile back at the airstrip, just as E-Dub is getting impatient waiting for the plane to arrive, he hears the sound of the plane approaching. He places a sinister smile on his face while rubbing his hands together. "This will be the coup of my career," he says to himself.

Just as the plane taxis to a stop, a truck pulls up to collect the artifacts. Once the plane comes to a complete stop, the door of the plane opens and two men emerge from the plane to check the perimeter. Seeing nothing out of the ordinary, they lower the ramp and begin unloading the crates. E-Dub is hoping his men don't jump the gun, and wait for the artifacts to be completely loaded into the truck. He likes his odds, he has twelve men to the eight men protecting the artifacts.

As the last crate is being placed in the back of the truck, E-Dub's men emerge from their hiding places only to fall flat on their faces. "What the hell," shouts E-Dub from his hiding place. The shots fired were quiet yet accurate, and each one of his men has been subdued. As Cockroach and his men emerge from their hiding places to check on the band of thieves, E-Dub leaves his hiding place and heads to his vehicle. He believes he is unseen as everyone is occupied taking care of his band of thieves. "I will not lose," he shouts as he heads to his car. "I will have to hijack the truck with the artifacts in it myself! It's a good thing I planted those tire spikes on the road before I got here!"

Just as he opens the door to the car, he hears a familiar voice, "Not so fast Sidewinder." As he reaches for the gun on his hip, the voice speaks again, "Unless you want to hear from the twins, I suggest you place both your hands in the air."

Knowing how deadly accurate his nemesis is, he does as he's told and turns in the direction of the voice. "I am so tired of you dogging my every move," he hisses.

"I believe this will be the last encounter that we have," replies Sylvia.

"I wouldn't be so sure of that," Sidewinder counters.

"And why is that?"

"I will not be so foolish as to tell you how I plan to get out of this!"

"If you think you can, go for it," Sylvia states in a deadly calm voice.

Sidewinder touches the palm of his right hand with two fingers, and shots ring out from Sylvia's right. Her right thigh is hit by one of the bullets and she falls to her knees, yet she manages to get off a shot. The round hits him in his right shoulder, yet he remains standing. "You little bitch,"
186

he says between clinched teeth as he reaches for his gun with his left hand. Sylvia lets another round fly, and this time she hits him dead between the eyes. He falls to his knees with a look of disbelief on his face before falling face down on the ground

Cockroach enters the hanger at that moment. "Snake Chaser," he calls out.

"Here."

He walks around the vehicle and sees her struggling to get to her feet. "Damn it, stay down!"

"It's a flesh wound, I can still walk."

"You are way too hard-headed for your own good. Let me help you."

"Fine," she says as she places her right arm around his shoulder. He helps her to stand, and together they walk to the waiting vehicle. All of the thieves have been bound, and loaded in the back of the truck. "I need to get bandaged up and over to the palace," she states as he helps her inside.

"Not a problem. We're headed to the palace anyway to lend our help to the security team there if anything out of the ordinary arises. However, before we leave I need to bag the trash," he states as he looks at Sidewinder lying on the ground.

"I can't be seen at the palace. You'll have to let me out before we get there."

"How do you propose to get there with a bullet hole in your leg?"

"I have a rabbit hole close to the palace. Drop me off there. I can patch myself up, and then make it to the palace on my own." She sees he's ready to protest. "Are you sure you want to battle me on this?"

He sighs, and gives in for he knows how pig-headed she can be. "Fine. Have it your way." He gets her settled in the truck, and then returns to tie up Sidewinder and alert Rock that the body is available for pick up.

"Thanks for handling this for me," states Rock on the other end of the phone. "I take of the body and the story surrounding his death so that no one knows of your involvement," he adds unaware that Marquise and the other agents already know of his involvement.

Preparing

Marquise, GL, and E&J gather their gear together as they wait for Czar to emerge from her room. She has finished packing, but needs a minute to get her nerves under control. Once she feels calm, she joins them in the living area. "Ready boys?"

"We were waiting on you," replies Marquise.

"Then let's head out."

They make their way downstairs to the car waiting to take them to the palace. The ride there is relatively quiet as each is caught up in their own thoughts about what is about to take place. However, the quiet of the ride is interrupted as both Marquise's and Erik's phones go off at the same time. Zamora is not sure who's conversation she should follow as they answer their phones, so tries to listen to both conversations.

"Pathfinder."

"Cockroach. Sidewinder's down, and his henchmen are in custody. Will take them to the palace holding cell until after the press conference."

"Was it necessary?"

"Yes."

"Any casualties?"

"One. Snake Chaser. Minor hit."

"Shit. See you at the palace."

*****

"Excalibur."

"Snake Chaser. Mission complete. Sidewinder slithers no more."

"Not the desired outcome, but expected."

"No choice. Took one in the thigh."

"Serious?"

"No. Flesh wound. This will be our last communiqué before I leave the country. Good Luck."

Before he can say another word, the line goes dead.

*****

Both men turn to Zamora at the same time, and say, "Sidewinder's out of play."

"And Snake Chaser?"

"One hit in the thigh," replies E&J.

"Shit! She's okay though?"

"She says she's fine, but we won't be seeing her again."

Zamora nods her head, and sits back against the seat for the remainder of the ride to the palace. Upon their arrival, she is taken in through a private entrance that leads straight to the Queen's bed room. She freezes as she takes in her surroundings, the room is incredible. Marquise studies her as she takes in the décor and opulence of the room. He smiles as her eyes widen as they scan the sculptures and paintings and carpets. After a few moments, he touches her on her shoulder to capture her attention. "This room is amazing," she says on a whisper. "It's like a museum itself."

He chuckles at the amazement in her voice. "Well I suggest you get use to it since this will become your bedroom when you take up residence in the palace."

"I don't know if I could sleep in here. This room is huge."

"I think you'll get used to in time, but right now you need to relax and get ready for the press conference." Feeling overwhelmed, she agrees. He kisses her on the forehead, and takes his leave.

Zamora is lying on the bed trying to absorb the reality of her situation when she swears she hears a faint swish as though a door has been opened. She sits up, and sure enough she sees Sylvia entering the room. She is too stunned to say a word. Sylvia walks over to her, sits down beside her, and takes her hands in hers. "Czar, I know this is all new to you, but you were born into this. And while it may take you a minute to assimilate, you will do well in your role as princess. If at any time you need me, here's my direct contact number," she states as she passes her a business card. "I have watched you grow up into a wonderful woman, God bless you on this new journey in your life. I will remain on the grounds until you are recognized as the Princess and the rightful governing factor of the kingdom, and then I will be gone."

Czar gives her a great bear hug, and then releases her. "Thank you for all you have done for me. I will never forget you. God speed as you continue your life's journey, and may you one day find the peace you so desperately seek."

Sylvia leaves the same way that she came, and Czar lies back down to continue her meditation about the new journey she is about to embark on as Princess Zahara of Umboto. She is eternally grateful that she will have Marquise by her side during this journey.

*****

After placing his bags in the room he was given, he goes in search of GL and E&J to make sure that everything is set with security. They assure him that everything is all set, and that Cockroach and his crew have arrived. Satisfied that everything is as it should be, Marquise heads to his room to relax as well. After removing his shoes, he lies down on the bed and stares at the ceiling. This is the first moment that he has been able to reflect on the new path his life has taken. He spent so little time as an FBI agent before becoming engaged to Zamora or Zahara as he must now get use to calling her, and he will now become a prince to boot. While he understands he will be a prince in name only, he wonders just how much responsibility for the kingdom he will be asked to take on. Then the thought hits him, once he and Czar marry they will be crowned King and Queen. He instantly sits up in the bed, and wonders if Czar has come to this realization as well. "She probably hasn't otherwise she would have really freaked out," he says out loud to himself. "Damn, she still has me talking to myself."

"That's not entirely true," says a voice from a shadowed corner of the room. Marquise immediately jumps from the bed and grabs his weapon from the bed's nightstand. "Relax Pathfinder, it's only me," states the voice as the person moves into the light.

"Damn it Snake Chaser! You know I hate it when you do that!" He places the weapon back on the nightstand as she moves closer to him.

She chuckles before giving him a big bear hug. "Czar, has not come to the realization that she will indeed be queen when the two of you marry," states to his amazement. At the stunned look on his face, she states, "That is the only thing that would make her freak out at this point." She then adds, "When she does, she will indeed freak out, so you will need to be her rock until she accepts that fact. I have watched over her for many years now, but as of today I am entrusting her to your care so don't disappointment me," she smiles as the last words leave her mouth.

"I will not disappoint you for she is my world, has been since the day we met on that Georgia highway two years ago."

"Glad to hear it. She knows how to reach me if you find that you need my help, and if you don't want her to know I'm being summoned there is always Excalibur."

"Duly noted. God speed Snake Chaser. May you soon find the peace you are searching for." They embrace once more, Sylvia leaves the way she came and Marquise again lies down on the bed.

*****

Rock places a call to Zamora to let her know of outcome of the sting operation. When she answers the phone, he states, "Sidewinder slithers no more. Enjoy your newly found destiny, and know that if you ever need me I am just a phone call away."

"Thanks for the update," she begins. "I will keep you on speed dial," she adds. The line goes dead, and she lays back down on the bed.

Marquise gets a similar call from Rock, as well as, a warning, "Make sure you take good care of her. She has dealt with a lot of tragedy for one so young."

"I plan to cherish her to the end of my days," responds Marquise just before the line goes dead.

ReGina Crawford

The Unveiling

The time for the press conference arrives, and Zamora is dressed in her royal attire and nervous as hell. Her hands feel like icicles and her knees are shaky, but she knows that she must appear confident for her people. Marquise is nervous as well, however, he shows no outward signs of his nervousness. The butterflies in his stomach, though, are doing a number on him. He knows that Zamora will need all of his strength at the press conference, so he ignores them and sends for E&J and GL so that they may collectively escort Zamora to the area for the press conference.

Once they arrive at her room, the guards on duty announce their arrival. Zamora's ladies in waiting admit them into the room. "Wow," states Marquise in awe of how regal she looks. "You look stunning," he adds.

She smiles before saying, "You don't look so bad yourself."

Marquise hears the slight tremble in her voice, and walks over to her and takes her hands in his. He notes how cold they feel, and whispers to her, "Everything will be fine. I will be by your side the entire time. Relax."

She whispers in return, "I'm trying to relax, but this is a bit overwhelming."

"It's time Princess," states one of the guards.

Marquise, while still holding her hand, escorts her to the press conference with Erik and Giovanni following close behind. When they arrive at the podium, loud cheers ring out throughout the crowd and it takes quite some time to get them to settle down.

The Xaliifa is the first to speak. "As most of you are aware, Princess Zahara has returned and she has in her possession the Royal Artifacts of the ruling monarchy. We are gathered here today to unveil the artifacts, and offer proof that she is indeed the rightful heir to the throne. Once these facts have been established, she will immediately assume the role of Ruler of Umboto and we will all pledge our undying loyalty to her." The crowd again erupts into loud cheers and the priest must wait for them to become silent once again. "We will first present to you the artifacts and validate their authenticity, and then the Princess will undergo the blood test to authenticate the blood line of the ruling class."

Zamora looks at Marquise wide-eyed as this is the first she has heard about a blood test. He returns her look with surprise in his face as well since he too was unaware of the blood test. However, they keep their silence so as not to disrupt the proceedings.

"After all facts have been verified, then there will be a short ten minute question and answer session with the Princess," states the Xaliifa. After the mumblings quiet down after that announcement, the Xaliifa continues, "The Princess has a lot to catch up on, so that is all the time that she can spare today. However, there will be other opportunities in the near future for some of you to talk with her at length."

The Xaliifa steps away from the podium, and Erik and the tribe's master art craftsmen step to the podium. "Greetings," begins Erik, "I am Erik Jackson, an art historian from the United States. I authenticated the artifacts while they were still in the US, and I will assist Zarie, your master arts craftsman, in authenticating the artifacts today. I can assure you that the artifacts are indeed genuine, and my findings will be proven in this room today."

"Let us begin," states Zarie. The two men then walk to each of the cases housing the royal artifacts, and Zarie inspects the two most important pieces, The Elephant Mask of the First King and The Fertility Doll of the First Queen. For these two artifacts ensure the wisdom and strength of the kingdom, and the kingdom's prosperity. After a careful and through inspection of the mask, Zarie announces, "The mask has the correct form and color of our tribe, and the wood is indeed authentic." A round of cheers is heard from the crowd as he moves on to the doll. Again he does a careful and through inspection of the shape, color, and materials of the sculpture before announcing, "The doll too is authentic." Cheers are once again heard from the crowd.

Once the crowd quiets, the kingdom doctor arrives to draw Zamora's blood and perform the test necessary to validate her blood line. The crowd remains quiet while the doctor places the blood on the slide and views it under the microscope. It is a nerve racking two minutes before he lifts his head and announces that Zamora does indeed have the blood markers of the royal family, and the crowd again begins cheering loudly.

After the crowd has quieted, the Xaliifa moves to the podium, "I now present to the Kingdom of Umboto Princess Zahara Umboto, rightful ruler of the tribe. And her chosen life mate Marquise McMillian."

The crowd remains quiet as they move to the podium. Zamora is the first to speak, "Greetings Umboto Kingdom. It is with humble pride that I stand before you accepting my role as your Princess. I know my parents must have loved you all very much for they went to great lengths and make great sacrifices to ensure that one day I would be the head of the kingdom." She pauses as the crowd erupts into cheers once again. "I pledge to uphold the beliefs and teachings of our ancestors, and vow to ensure the prosperity of the tribe." She turns to Marquise before addressing the crowd again. "I most humbly request that the tribe accept Marquise McMillian as my life mate and Prince of the Umboto Kingdom." She squeezes his hand and prompts him to speak to the people.

"Greetings Umboto Kingdom. I too stand before you with humble pride as the chosen life mate of your Princess. I pledge my life to her and the members of this tribe as her chosen Prince," he states as he looks at her lovingly. The crowd is pleased, and once again erupts into cheers.

The Xaliifa moves to the podium to quiet the crowd, and acknowledges one of the reporters who has their hand raised to ask a question.

"I see the Princess is wearing the royal engagement ring, when will the wedding ceremony take place?"

"The ceremony will take place in one week's time," responds the Xaliifa. Zamora and Marquise fight hard to maintain their composure with his announcement as they were unaware that the wedding ceremony would take place so quickly.

"Will the ceremonial crowning them King and Queen take place at the same time," asks the same reporter.

"Yes, the ceremonial crowning will take place directly after the wedding ceremony." Again Zamora and Marquise are stunned. Zamora's hand in Marquise's goes as cold as ice, and he gives it a reassuring squeeze.

"How did the Princess and the future Prince meet," asks another reporter.

The Xaliifa steps aside to let the couple answer the question. Marquise answers as he feels Zamora inability to speak at the moment. "We met in America right after Princess Zahara's grandmother's passing. He feels Zamora's slight flinch at hearing him address her as Princess Zahara. "I was immediately lost in the brightness and sincerity of her soul," he continues. "And amazingly enough, she was immediately enamored of me as well. We believe that we are soul mates and that our initial encounter was not one of chance, but one of divine design," he adds.

Zamora's strength is renewed by Marquise's words, as well as, his touch. "Your future King is quite right," she states as she finds her voice. "I believe that the Gods and my parents are responsible for our initial meeting, and will bless our union."

"We have heard rumblings about an attempt to steal the royal artifacts. Were they in any danger of being stolen and sold on the black market," asks a third reporter.

"We have heard the rumblings as well. I assure you that the artifacts were never in any danger as they have been in palace under guard for over a month," responds Zamora.

"You fraud," shouts someone from the crowd. "You led us to believe that you arrived in country first!" Everyone in the crowd turns in the direction of the voice to find one of the high ranking members of the Gamboto tribe. When he notices everyone looking in his direction, he yells, "What are you all looking at?" However, before he can say another word, he is surrounded by members of the Umboto Royal Guard. They take him into custody, and escort him from the room.

Once the commotion dies down, the Xaliifa informs the crowd that the Princess will take one more question before the press conference comes to a close.

"How soon can we expect an heir to the throne," asks yet another reporter.

"Of that we are unsure," replies Zamora as she turns and smiles at Marquise. "However, I believe your future King will make that his number one priority."

"It will be my honorable duty to provide the kingdom with the next heir to the throne, and I never shirk my duty," adds Marquise.

The crowd erupts into laughter, and the press conference is brought to a close. Once the crowd has been escorted out of the throne room, Marquise and Zamora take their seats on the throne to process the information that they received at the conference.

Rules and Repercussions

"It seems we will become husband and wife and King and Queen all in a week's time," states Marquise.

"So it seems," responds Zamora somewhat lost in thought. However, she quickly returns her focus to Marquise, "Did it dawn on you that we would be crowned King and Queen after our marriage?"

"Not until about an hour ago," he answers. "I figured it hadn't occurred to you, and I am greatly impressed that you held yourself together at the announcement during the press conference."

"It took everything in me not to freak out when the Xaliifa made that bit of news known. It was one thing to have it announced that we would be married within a week, but to hear that I would also be crowned Queen on the same day was definitely a shocker."

"I know," says Marquise, "but I think we did very well in our reactions to the news."

"Yes, you did indeed do very well," states the Xaliifa as he enters the room. He notices Zamora is about to speak and holds up a hand to stifle the flow of words he knows she's dying to unleash. As she tilts her head in question, he states, "You are just like your mother in temperament, so I know you are dying to blister my ears for not informing you of the upcoming ceremonies. However, the announcements were made in the manner they were made as a test of your true strength and ability to rule this kingdom. I must say that you both passed with flying colors, as they say in America."

"Since I am not well versed in the traditions of the kingdom, I am going to let this one slide, however, all future major announcements had better be made to me in private," states Zamora.

"Yes Princess Zahara."

"That is something else I will have to get use to," Zamora states. At the Xaliifa's raised eyebrow, she adds, "Being addressed as Zahara instead of Zamora."

"Ahh, yes," responds the priest. "I think the adjustment will be easy since no one other than perhaps your prince will slip up and address you as Zamora." Both Marquise and Zamora nod in agreement. "There is much work to be done in less than a week, so I must be on my way. I suggest you two get as much rest as you can in the meantime."

"Wait," Zamora nearly shouts. When the priest pauses and turns back to her, she asks, "What happened to the gentlemen who called me a fraud at the press conference?"

"He was escorted to the tribal council holding cell, and he and the Gamboto tribe will be dealt with at the council meeting that will take place tomorrow. You both will be present, but only the Princess will be allowed to speak." With that being said, he again turns and heads out of the room.

"Your first official duty as Princess." Zamora simply glares at Marquise. He chuckles as he asks, "What did I say?" She bursts out laughing with him. "That's my girl," he says before rising from his chair to offer her his hand to help her up from hers. "Go get some rest. We'll deal with the tribal council issue later." She nods and heads to her room. The two members of the royal guard assigned to her follow in behind her as she walks down the hall to her room.

Marquise also heads to his room, but not to relax. He places a call to Rock to find out if the US Government will have any say so in the punishment of Enrique's henchmen since they did attack a US envoy. He is told that the US will not participate in the trial and punishment of the criminals as they are all members of the Gamboto tribe and none of his men were injured. Marquise ends the call with Rock, and lies down on the bed. "I'll be glad when this mission is over," he states out loud before closing his eyes.

*****

Zamora enters her room to find her ladies-in-waiting waiting for her. They have already turned down the bed, and there is a tray with hot tea on it waiting for her. "Your Grace," they say in unison as they curtsy as she enters the room.

"Aster. Bella. Thanks for the tea, but I think I can take care if everything else from here."

"Are you sure Your Grace," asks Aster who seems to be the head of this two woman team.

"I'm sure," she responds. "Go tend to your other duties in the palace."

The ladies leave, and Zamora strips down before climbing to the middle of the bed tea in hand. Feeling overloaded, she decides that she will not think of anything. She will drink her tea and take a nap. Everything will still be here when she wakes up.

*****

Several hours later, they both wake up and make their way to the throne room to call all the tribal leaders together to determine what course of action they should take at the Tribal Council tomorrow.

Each of them walks into the throne room at the same time. "Your Grace," states Marquise while bowing to her. At her raised eyebrow, he simply smiles his devastating smile at her. She simply shakes her head at him. "Shall we summon the tribal leaders to discuss tomorrow's proceedings?"

"Are you trying to read my mind?"

"I wouldn't dare," he replies while unleashing that smile.

"I'll deal with you later," she chuckles. "Let's get the business at hand done." She calls for the tribal leaders and once they have all arrived, they get down to the business at hand.

"As you all know, the Gamboto tribe has been trying to gain control of our kingdom for quite some time, and their latest attempts have lead to the deaths of several people," begins Zamora. "The US Government has chosen not to participate in the proceedings despite the fact that one of their citizens and officials was killed during this latest coup since he was actually killed by their own people," she adds. "So, we are left with the task of deciding what should be done with the men that are currently in custody, and what sanctions should be imposed against the Gamboto Kingdom," she continues. "As I am not well versed in tribal laws, I will follow the recommendations of the leaders," she concludes.

The Elder leader speaks first, "At this point we cannot prove that the Gambotos caused the plane crash that killed the King and Queen, nor can we prove that they killed Zarif and Zarina." He notices the surprised look on Zamora's face, and addresses her directly, "Yes, we knew that Zarif and Zarina left country with you, however, we did not know where you were. We thought that it was in everyone's best interest that your location be kept secret. When they returned two years ago, it was at their request since they knew the terms surrounding your assumption of the throne. They thought that you would need time to meet your future life mate, and wanted you to have sufficient time to do so. Their subsequent death was not foreseen, and actually left us at a loss as to how to get you back in country. So when it was rumored that you were here posing as the heir of

Zarif and Zarina, we were unsure of how to proceed since we didn't know how much you knew of your true identity. We were forced to stand on the sideline, and watch the events play out." He finishes, and the room is quiet as Zamora processes all of what she has just heard.

Marquise takes both her hands in his, and forces her to look into his eyes. "I know that came as a shock to you, and I'm sure other things will be revealed that will come as a shock to you as well. However, I'm going to need you to maintain your composure, and I know that you can do it," he begins. "You are a highly trained FBI agent, so you know how to keep your feelings hidden," he continues. "I know this is more personal to you than any case you've been on, but when out in public you will have to rely on your training to not let your feelings show," he further adds.

"I know. I guess that so much has happened in such a short period of time that I'm feeling out of my element at the moment. And on top of it, I have a wedding to plan."

The Xaliifa speaks up at that moment, "The wedding plans are all set. All you have to do is learn what to do when, and show up."

"Really?"

"Really, so don't worry about that. Concentrate on dealing with the Gambotos, and getting to know your people."

She takes a few deep breaths, and feels her composure return. "Okay. I'm fine now. Let's determine what we feel should be the repercussions for the crimes the Gambotos have committed against the Umbotos."

The Tribal Council

"As I was saying," the elder begins again, "The only thing that we can prove is that Gambotos tried to assassinate Princess Zahara in the market place based on the footage that was obtained that day. We can also prove that members of their tribe tried to hi-jack the artifacts at the airstrip, however, we can't prove that the leaders of the tribe knew about the hi-jacking," he pauses as he continues his thoughts privately. "Unless we can get the ones in custody to talk."

"Do you think that's likely to happen with the Gamboto leaders present," asks Marquise.

"More than likely, it won't happen," responds one of the other leaders. "However, we might be able to question them without their leaders present."

"You know that is not the way of the tribal council," states the elder.

"What if the Gambotos decide that they want to disengage themselves from their tribal members? Then they don't have to be present when we question them as they will be declared renegades."

"And as much trouble as they're facing with these attempts on the life of a princess, and artifact theft, they may not want to take their chances facing the tribal council," states the elder.

205

Before another word can be spoken, there is a knock on the door. One of the guards at the door opens it, and in steps the messenger from the Gamboto tribe with an envelope for the tribal leaders. The elder takes and opens the envelope and reads its contents out loud.

> *The King and Queen, as well as, the Tribal Leaders*
> *of the Gamboto Tribe have disengaged ourselves*
> *from the members of our tribe that have committed*
> *crimes against the Kingdom of Umboto. We will not*
> *interfere with whatever punishments are doled out to*
> *them, nor do we wish the Kingdom of Gamboto to be*
> *held responsible for their actions for they did not act*
> *on directive from the King or Queen or any of our*
> *tribal leaders.*
>
> *King and Queen Gamboto*

"Well it seems the Gambotos have given us the opening we need to find out the truth about our suspicions," states Marquise.

"Indeed it does," comments Zamora. "So, with this new turn of events, what are our next steps?"

"We will present this missive to the Tribal Council, and then we will be given to the opportunity to question the prisoners without inference from the Gambotos," states the elder. "I will compose a list of grievances that we will present to the council, and then the proceedings will begin. Depending on the answers we receive, the council will then determine if the Gambotos should be tried as well. I suggest we all get a good night's sleep for tomorrow will be a long and trying day. I will see you all in the morning."

With his parting the words, the Tribal Leaders leave the throne room leaving Zamora and Marquise alone. He takes her in his arms and holds her in silence for quite a while. He then lifts her head, kisses her on the forehead, then tells her, "It will be a long night without you next to me. In fact it will be a long week without you next to me."

"I know what you mean," she replies. "In the beginning I thought that a week was way too short a time for us to get married, but now it's feeling like an eternity."

The look in her eyes is almost his undoing, so he states, "Let me walk you to your door so you can get a good night's rest. The elder is right, tomorrow will be a long and trying day, and if I answer the call in your eyes right now it will be a very long night that won't leave you at your best for tomorrow." She smiles a seductive smile his way, and he turns her towards the door. "Behave yourself! Let's go," he states as he ushers her to the door. At the door to her room, he once again kisses her forehead before saying, "I love you."

"I love you too."

He opens her door, ushers her inside, and then heads down the hall to his own room.

*****

The next morning, the Tribal Council assembles, and the Umboto Leaders present them with the letter from the Gambotos, as well as, the list of offenses committed by the men in custody and the alleged offenses committed by the Gambotos. The council brings forth the prisoners and questions them about their activities and the role the Gamboto's leaders played in those activities. When the prisoners find out that the Gamboto leaders had disengaged themselves from them, they wasted no time at all detailing all the misdeeds they committed and the role the King, Queen, and their advisors played in all those deeds. They know that their fate is sealed anyway, so they have no qualms about taking down the people that have left them to the hangman's noose.

Once the council has the information that it needs, it wastes no time sending for the heads of the Gamboto Kingdom.

The King and Queen are summoned before the council first. As they enter the room, the King says rather testily, "What is the meaning of this? We officially disengaged ourselves from the men you have in custody. We had no knowledge of their activities." The Queen nods her head in agreement at his side.

"Unfortunately, your countrymen have told the council otherwise. They even provided us with documents and recordings that substantiate their claims," states the head of the Tribal Council. "So, I suggest you take the heat out of your voice, and you and your Queen take a seat." The King and Queen are both stunned, and immediately take their seats. "The evidence that we have in our possession is very condemning, and could lead to your beheading, however, the council has voted against putting you on trial. Since you cannot be stripped of your titles, the council has decided that you will be confined to your kingdom for the remainder of your days on this earth. While you will maintain the title of King and Queen, your kingdom will now be governed by the Tribal Council in pretty much the same way the Umboto Kingdom has been governed the past twenty-eight years. If you are unwilling to accept these terms, we will have no choice but to have a formal trial at which you will be found guilty and sentenced to death. Do you need time to decide how you would like to proceed?"

Without hesitation, the King responds, "We accept the punishment and do not request a trial." The Queen doesn't say a word, but does nod her head in agreement.

"Now as for your Tribal Leaders, they will be imprisoned for life. You should also know that any more antics by either of you will make this arrangement null and void and you will face the most severe punishment available."

"We understand, and thank you for sparing our lives," states the King.

208

"Might I ask a question," interjects the Queen.

The King looks at her as though she has grown an extra head, but she ignores him and focuses her attention on the leader of the Tribal Council who answers her. "Yes, you may."

"What about our children?"

"Your children will be watched very carefully, and if they attempt to embark on any of the antics that you two have employed they will face the same punishment as their parents."

"Understood," replies the King as he looks at his wife with annoyance.

"Then I call this Tribal Council adjourned," states the Tribal Council Leader.

Royal Passion

Once they return to the palace, Marquise escorts Zamora to the throne room, and gathers her into a tight embrace. He kisses the top of her head before whispering in her ear, "The mission is over. Now it is time for us to focus on the ceremony, and us becoming husband and wife." He leans back so that he may look directly into her eyes before saying, "I love you heart, body, and soul."

"I love you heart, body, and soul," she returns with the shimmer of tears in her eyes. She lays her head on his chest, and gives him a quick squeeze before returning her eyes to his. "Marquise," she whispers, "I'm scared." He quirks an eyebrow at her, and she continues, "I have no idea what I'm supposed to do during the ceremony, and I would hate to anger the people of my country by doing something I shouldn't."

"I'm sure we will both receive detailed instructions on everything that will take place during the ceremony," he replies. "I think the hardest thing for me will be not being able to see you, or hold you, or make love to you." He feels her body shiver and realizes the effect his words have had on her, and that realization only heightens his desire. "I think I should escort you back to your room before we both find ourselves sprawled out in the middle of this carpet," he states with a smile. Her eyes darken with passion, and her lips part as her breathing gets a little heavier. "Uhn't Uh," he begins as he turns her loose, and turns her toward the door. "I'm taking your little temptress self to your room," he adds just before he opens the door to the throne room. At her door he, he looks her in her eyes, and says, "I suggest you get as much rest as you can this week because after the ceremony you won't get much." With a wink and a smile he takes off down the hall.

Zamora is left standing there shivering in her desire to make love to her man, and makes plans to make him pay for this little interlude as soon as they are alone again.

*****

The next seven days are a whirlwind of activity as Marquise and Zamora are prepared for the ceremony and their roles as King and Queen. They only see each other in passing as they are shuffled from one meeting to another, and they are so exhausted at the end of the day that they fall into a deep sleep every night. Finally the day of the ceremony arrives, and each wakes with a smile on their face in anticipation of the night to come.

The wedding guests are assembled in the throne room awaiting their arrival. First enters Marquise dressed in the traditional robes of the King. Next enters Zamora also dressed in traditional robes. The Xaliifa performs the ceremony uniting them in marriage followed by the ceremony to crown them as King and Queen of Umboto. As the last words are spoken, the crowd erupts into loud cheers and Zamora and Marquise bow to their people. The celebration begins as music begins to play, and massive amounts of food are placed on tables around the room. They are congratulated by just about everyone in attendance, and never have a moment alone. However, they are overjoyed by the ready acceptance of the people of Umboto of their new roles as King and Queen. Several hours later, the people start to depart and the celebration winds down, and it is at this point that Marquise and Zamora are escorted from the room to be prepped for the royal honeymoon.

*****

ReGina Crawford

An hour later, Marquise is directed to a panel inside his room and his valet places his hand on the crest in the center of the panel. The panel quietly slides open, and the valet takes his leave. Marquise walks through the opening to find himself in the Queen's room, and he finds the Queen standing in the middle of the room looking divine in a whisper thin robe. He slowly walks over to her, and makes a complete circle around her without saying a word. Once he is facing her again, he simply stands there admiring her beauty.

Following the instructions she was given, Zamora walks over to a table, that Marquise didn't even notice when he walked in the room, and picks up two glasses. She extends one of the glasses in his direction, and without saying a word he takes the glass from her hand. The heat from their fingers barely caressing causes both of them to quickly sip from their glasses. Zamora is the first to set down her glass, and then she walks in the direction of her bed while letting the robe glide from her body. Marquise is mesmerized and quickly follows behind her, catching up to her just as she reaches the platform the bed is sitting on. Unable to hold out any longer, he kisses her for all he's worth and she allows herself to drown in the passion of his kiss. The need to breathe is the only thing that causes him to break the kiss, at which point he picks her up and carries her the rest of the way to the bed. "I want this night to be perfect for you," he states as he places her in the center of the bed. "But right now, I need this. Been craving this," he adds just before he raises her hips to his lips and feasts like a man too long deprived.

Zamora is speechless at first, however, as the sensations he's creating with his lips and tongue roll through her body, she finds her voice, "Marquise," she says through gritted teeth, "Yes. . . I've missed . . . the way . . . you love me . . . like this." Shortly thereafter, her orgasm crashes down on her with the force of a tidal wave, and she screams his name.

As she lays there riding out the last waves of her climax, Marquise disrobes and rejoins her on the bed, "I'm sorry for making you cum so quickly, but I needed to taste you," he states just before he gathers her in his arms and kisses her deeply.

Heart Body and Soul

Zamora, determined to give as good as she gets, uses the intensity of the kiss to flip Marquise on his back and take control. Breathless from the kiss, Marquise is easily overpowered and unable to stop Zamora from taking his steel hard manhood into her mouth. His upper body jerks up off the bed at the first feel of her mouth, and she gives him a look that tells him not to interrupt her. So he leans back on his elbows and watches her as she makes love to him with her mouth. He is powerless to stop her as he reaches his own orgasm, and simply screams her name with his release. She climbs back up his body so that they are face to face, and smiles as she says, "I've been craving you as well," before kissing him.

Once he's recovered from her loving, he flips her on back and breaks the kiss. "That wasn't supposed to happen," he says with a slight frown on his face.

She gives him a quick kiss before stating, "Yes it was, but don't worry I was told that the drink we drank when you came in here would give you the stamina to make up for all the time we've been apart."

"What," he nearly yells.

Unable to resist, Zamora laughs before saying, "One of my ladies in waiting told me that the drink would temporarily give me the power to have my way with you, but once the full effect kicked in that I should be ready for a long night."

"So you've drugged me, have you," asks Marquise.

"Actually, I've drugged us both, and I can't wait for it to take effect."

Just as the words leave her lips, Marquise feels the power of the drug take over. His manhood instantly awakens, and he wastes no time plunging into the wet hot flesh he's been craving for a week. The feel of her womanly core surrounding him, pulsating around him, momentarily takes his breath away, and he stays perfectly still. He stares into her face until her eyes open, as she closed them when he entered her, "I love you," he says with such sincerity that tears form in her eyes.

"I love you too," she whispers just as the drug takes over her body and her inners walls begin squeezing him until he is compelled to make love to her with long deep strokes that cause moans to erupt from deep in her throat. Before she knows it she's screaming his name as another orgasm washes over her causing her body to tremble uncontrollably. "I'm not . . . going . . . to survive . . . if every . . . orgasm . . . is going . . . to be . . . like this," she's barely able to get out as he picks up the speed of his strokes one her trembling stops.

"That . . .makes . . . two . . . of us," Marquise barely gets out as his body seems to have a mind of its own and he makes love to her for all he's worth.

Several hours and an unknown number of orgasms later, Marquise looks into Zamora's eyes and says, "If you weren't on the pill, I would say without a doubt that you became pregnant tonight."

"The drug we took was a fertility drug, so pill or no pill I would say I probably am pregnant." She laughs at the shocked look on his face after her statement. However, her laughter dies quickly as he enters her body again, and he begins the deep powerful stroking that she loves.

Upcoming works from the author:

Snake Chaser

For those of you who have expressed a love for Sylvia, and want to hear her whole story.

Icing On The Cake

For those of you who have asked what happened to Jade and Kyle, and Ebony and Kendrick.